Treasure this masterpiece!

The Treasure Hunt

With compliments from
Rolic Oboh

Rolic Oboh

Strategic Book Publishing and Rights Co.

Strategic Book Publishing and Rights Co., LLC
USA | Singapore

For information about special discounts for bulk purchases, please contact Strategic Book Publishing and Rights Co. Special Sales, at bookorder@sbpra.net.

ISBN: 978-1-63135-686-5

Book Design: Suzanne Kelly

Acknowledgements

This book is dedicated to all school administrators, teachers and students, especially to Government College Ughelli, class of '70.

Special thanks also to my wife and children for putting up with me, and to my editor and publisher for their support and encouragement.

R. O.
October 2014

CHAPTER 1

Except for the somnolent Bede Olo inside, the Sapele House dormitory block was quiet and deserted. On his bed inside what formerly was the Common Room, Bede's mind flickered in a trance-like sleep. Sometimes he was awake, his consciousness seemingly far off, and his eyes opened intermittently. Other times he was deeply asleep, his eyes glazed over and partially covered with thick, fleshy eyelids.

Like his dormitory inmates, Bede ought to have been at the soccer field to watch the most exciting match of the year. He was not thrilled by the sport, so he surreptitiously stayed back to enjoy his lazy afternoon.

At about 4:15 p.m. and over a hundred yards away, the match kicked off. There was now a permanent lull in all conversation as spectators and players alike riveted their attention on the ball.

At that moment, Bede could hear birdcalls and the wind blowing through the acacia and frangipani trees and hibiscus shrubs all around the block. Then, the breeze drifted inside the common room, spinning and trussing him like a lasso. Bede turned over and drifted off again to another round of deep sleep.

A stealthy old man approached Bede's bedside furtively. Small and shrunken, his five-foot-six-inch frame was swathed in an old homespun loincloth and topped by a threadbare danshiki. The lines of age and exertion marked his hollow, long face and bony limbs. Death haunted him, like a subject lifted out of a painting by Goya, though in his eyes, there burned a fierce determination and a desperate hope.

From the goatskin pouch he carried, he hurriedly brought out a freshly cut blade of lemongrass. Positioning himself near the sleeping boy, he made a neat incision on the side of one of the boy's feet with the grass. Blood oozed out of the cut, and the old man wiped it dry with a piece of dirty old rag. He immediately stopped the bleeding, and then replaced both the blade of grass and the dirty old rag in his pouch. After this was done he sailed out of the room, his eyes gleaming with satisfaction.

John Austin, principal of Government College, shifted his bulky self on his chair atop the pavilion. His blue eyes squinted afar at the point of play in the soccer field below. The ball only a moment ago ricocheted off the Warri House goalpost and missed the net by mere inches.

Ace left forward, Daniel Oke of School House, masterfully prevented the ball from going out of play. He quickly tipped the ball back towards the Warri House goal line, while four opposing defenders swooped on him.

John Austin usually liked to catch the drama of every soccer match as it unfolded. For that he used his binoculars, like a military field commander that he once was. Today, he forgot to bring them with him, so he asked the head of school (or senior prefect) to send a junior student to retrieve them. But that was a long time ago! He grimaced and looked furiously all around. The head of school was nowhere near on the pavilion.

Christopher Nomo, the playful class-one boy he was, cheerfully hopscotched his way on imaginary squares towards the principal's staff quarters. On his way back to the soccer field, he planned to take a detour through a bush path near a broken-down side of the school's perimeter fence. He would sprint at intervals and arrive at the pavilion breathless. That way, the head of school would think he actually ran all the way to and from the principal's staff quarters in order to fetch the binoculars.

Upon arrival at the principal's staff quarters, however, Christopher did not immediately find the butler to give him the binoculars. It took some time before the butler, who had gone into his own room in the boy's quarters, came round to give Christopher the binoculars.

As the butler handed the binoculars to him, Christopher peeped through the slightly opened door, and he had a quick glimpse of a cavernous sitting room. He saw a plush settee and a high wall lined with statuettes in gilded niches. He wished he could go inside the sitting room just to wander among its rich furniture, the likes of which he had not seen anywhere before.

Christopher recalled the stories told by the senior students about the principal. John Austin was a widower without children who reputedly spent much of his wealth acquiring masterpiece paintings and sculptures. Christopher often heard the senior students mention some names in the principal's art and literary collection, like Gauguin, Picasso, Flaubert, Monet, and Rodin, many of whom he never heard of, but he knew one thing said about the principal was certain: he had a complete art gallery and extensive literary collection in his house. It was one of the reasons he taught the only classical art course for students in forms three to six at the school.

Christopher's favourite subject was art. He could draw very well, like a real picture, but he did not yet know about the masters, whom he yearned to learn about and discover the secret of their talent. For that, he would have to wait till he was in Class Three, going by the school's curriculum. Yet, now was a golden opportunity to satisfy his curiosity by browsing at Mr. Austin's rich art collection. Thinking about browsing the principal's art collection reminded Christopher that he had already taken too long to fetch the binoculars, so he scurried off towards the bush path leading to the soccer field, while holding the binoculars jauntily in his right hand.

CHAPTER 2

In the distance, the din of boisterous cheer rose. A climax was imminent, but now there was a momentary lull. Christopher hurried along the bush path at a throttle towards the field. He did not even see the face of the old man in the dirty worn-out clothes, whom he nearly bumped into as both he and the old man kept going their separate ways. The old man furtively turned round afterward to see if the fast little boy who almost bumped into him had shown any curiosity. No! The little rascal was gone! The old man breathed a sigh of relief, but wished for no further such encounter as he too hurried away from the scene. Soon, he crossed a break in the perimeter fence and disappeared into the forest.

At the precise moment the loud cheering reached a crescendo, Stanley Osa neared the goal line and missed the goal he ought to have scored. Immediately, there followed a sharp backlash from the spectators and players alike.

There was a loud murmur and a welter of disappointed, disapproving hisses, grunts and outcries. It was just as well no one called out his usual nicknames, *comic footballer* or *The Rolling Stone* or *chief fowler*. Stanley, however, shrivelled into himself and wished he could disappear from the face of the earth.

Mr. John Austin, sweating profusely, raised his hands in dismay. He was shocked by this anticlimax early in the match. A keen golfer, he ruefully drew a comparison between the lost goal and a golfer's moment of triumph turned to dismay when he failed to putt the ball in the hole.

Warri House was clearly reverting to being the underdog. *That bewildering Stanley Osa could prove to be the bane of School House!* John Austin concluded as he reached into his pocket case for one of his cigars.

Christopher appeared at the edge of the huge clearing nestling four soccer fields as the cheering subsided. The farthest was where the match was being played. He was fascinated by the smallness of the people far away either playing or watching the match. Their diminished sizes made him recall the Lilliputians of *Gulliver's Travels* with a jest. And then he thought of the binoculars in his hand.

The novelty of trying out the field glasses appealed so much to him, his big eyes shone with glee. Before long, he held the binoculars to his eyes and excitedly swung all around to cover the entire field of play a hundred yards away.

Sunlight, screened off from entering and illuminating the binoculars, bounced off the object lenses, and the glare reported their use to Mr. John Austin far away atop the pavilion.

An idiot is using my binoculars, Austin thought to himself. He grimaced, looked all round, and gazed out to where the glare came from.

The glare far away continued its tell-tale of the binoculars misuse judging by the wildly changing direction. For one brief moment, they stared Mr. John Austin right in the face, and the portly expatriate school principal instinctively flinched.

I'd like to rusticate this idiot who's amusing himself with my binoculars, while I sit here waiting for them! he exasperatedly thought, half rising from his chair then sitting back down again. He reached inside the pocket of his favourite beige slacks for a handkerchief and mopped sweat off his now pale face.

CHAPTER 3

"Your binoculars, sir!" Gerald Egbe said, bending curtly to hand over the principal's field glasses to him. The six-foot-two head of school, with a torso like Charles Atlas, was the most beloved student on the campus. The white singlet and black shorts he wore, which were customary for after-class hours in the afternoons, especially for siesta and for sports, merely detailed his splendid physique.

Right then, however, John Austin was feeling anything but amiable adoration for his handpicked head of school (or senior prefect). "I'll say, it's about time!" he bellowed.

Gerald knew better than to argue with his angry school principal, or advance reasons in his own defence. He merely smiled a toothless smile back and waited his cue to leave.

But John Austin wasn't quite finished yet. "Where did you send for them—the moon?"

Again, Gerald was silent and responded with the same awkward smile. Just then, the fat-bottomed games master tapped Gerald on the shoulder and whispered something to him. Gerald's eyes arched up slightly, but at the time he couldn't give much attention to what the games master was saying to him.

At first, when handed his binoculars, Mr. Austin handled them like he would his handkerchief if inadvertently dropped in the senior staff lavatory. After wiping them clean, he warmed to their use. The play in the field was intensifying.

"I was gonna say *we* should rusticate him, the boy you sent for my binoculars." John Austin accentuated the "we" like a newfound dialect. He was still talking to Gerald, who was momentarily distracted by what the games master was saying inaudibly to him, and did not answer.

"Say Jay!" Austin continued saying.

The cheering rose loudly. The ball shot past the Warri House goalpost missing the net by mere inches. The player who kicked it was soon booed by the disconsolate spectators. For once, it was not Stanley Osa who missed the golden opportunity to score a goal. This in fact provided a mighty doze of relief to Stanley and lent easy gait to his rickety legs as he ambled along in the play, his black shorts stirring in the sudden breeze.

John Austin soon turned around and realized why Gerald had not answered him. He glared at the duo that met his gaze. "What is this? Here I am talking to you, and you just stand there and don't even answer," he thundered as if the games master was not there.

As soon as John Austin turned to look at both of them, the games master scurried off, leaving only the head of school to receive the principal's thundering accusation.

"Preliminary reports reaching me indicate that there's one student missing from this arena."

"Not the one you sent for my binoculars, I hope?"

"No. No, sir."

"Well, find him!" the Principal growled.

Gerald was only too glad to leave his presence.

CHAPTER 4

The soccer match was intensifying again. Daniel Oke, School House's midfielder, was about to do a famous double take. Dodging and dribbling the ball past most of the Warri House defenders, he suddenly stopped short of the opposing team's goalpost with no room to shoot the ball past the goalkeeper. Steven Owho, the Warri House goalkeeper, initially taken in by surprise, was ranging close to Oke.

Daniel threw a feint to the left, but Steven blocked him. In a daring do, Daniel flew upwards, the ball firmly remaining between his two feet. While in midair, he twisted and somersaulted, and simultaneously, his feet sent the ball past the consternated goalkeeper. Steven, like a careening Shango (the god of NEPA) had his two hands grabbing at empty air. It was a goal!

The crowd of spectators went wild. Supporters of School House began to throw dry grass confetti onto the soccer field.

"Order!, order!" John Austin muttered under his breath. He wished he had a gavel with him, and the whole spectacle before him could be whipped into quiet conformity by his flogging it. He hated hooliganism in sports, and any behaviour foreshadowing it was unnerving for him. For that reason, he despised youthful exuberance. African youth, he since concluded, hid stress under a veneer of calmness but were more easily vexatious when stressed a little.

To John Austin's relief, the excitement soon died down, especially as the play resumed again. Warri House, the losing team, now changed their midfielder. Judging from this and the stern look on the faces of their players, there appeared to be a fresh resolve on the part of the team to not readily concede defeat to School House.

Perhaps the house master in charge of that team sent word round to his players, charging them to win the match unfailingly or else they could forget about returning to the dormitory that evening—where an irate house master would be waiting to give each player a piece of his mind.

Perhaps so, John Austin ruminated. "Win the match or don't come back to Warri House this evening!"

The loosing team may have been upbraided by the house master. *Just as well then*, John Austin thought to himself. *I, for one, would like to see a challenging match.*

A sudden stir behind him made John Austin turn around, frowning. The pavilion, whenever he was seated there, took on the discreet tranquillity of a Greek ruin, especially one under invasion by wide-eyed tourists. So, quite naturally, he resented this sudden commotion.

Three prefects lingered around him and the head of school wasn't with them, which made his frown deepen. They were shooing around a thin-faced man or boy nearby. The eyes were a boy's, but the other features of the body were those of an old man, or one hewn with age and exertion.

John Austin merely took in what he saw; he was not about to be distracted by it. He raised his hand mightily and gestured for the group of three prefects with the boy or man to move away to the extremity of the pavilion, far from him.

The leading prefect's determination to present what seemed to him a very pertinent matter disappeared, because of the hostile reception by the principal. He and the other two prefects turned around expectantly. They were met with stares from the other teachers and students on the pavilion that seemed to indicate just what the principal's gesture was saying. In other words, they should disappear!

Just like the restless mob in Shakespeare's Coriolanus, Samson Uwagwu, the leading prefect thought, *we are being driven out of this arena.* Then fresh resolve came to him. *After all*, he thought to himself, *here was a matter of life and death that just couldn't wait, and had to be told to the principal at once.*

He suggested the other prefects withdraw while he alone now advanced towards Mr. John Austin.

"Excuse me, sir." The hard lines formed around John Austin's mouth, Samson noticed, as he called for the principal's attention.

Surprisingly, those lines disappeared by the time the principal turned around fully to look at him straight in the eye. "Yes, what do you want?"

Samson met the principal's gaze without flinching. He didn't have the theatrical toothless smile that Gerald espoused. However, he was conscious of the stone in his chest, and he knew he wanted to quickly tell the principal what he had to say.

"There is a case of impersonation . . ." Samson spoke these words arrestingly and faltered. He had not thought all about what to say to the principal or even how to present it.

John Austin kept studious silence.

"Your excellency, I mean, sir . . . there's . . ."

John Austin cut Samson short. "Get Gerald for me, would you?"

The prefect bit his lower lip in exasperation and shame. Before he straightened himself up to join the others of his group, Gerald was beside him. Samson now breathed a sigh of relief, and his taut facial muscles began to relax. Gerald ignored him for the moment.

"You're not going to believe this, sir," Gerald told the principal, John Austin, who now cocked his ears to him.

John Austin turned to him with animation. "Believe what?"

"The missing boy was found, but he's changed to a sixty-year-old man."

John Austin burst into a deep raucous laughter, more because of the seriousness with which Gerald spoke to him than what actually the prefect said.

"Tell me another one, Jay," Austin said incredulously, laughing again loudly. "Is this some of your African voodoo stuff?"

CHAPTER 5

Something stirred deeply inside Stanley Osa the moment Daniel Oke scored the first goal for School House in the match, especially because of the ovation it attracted. He considered matters afresh. In appearance, Daniel Oke was frailer looking than he Stanley Osa, yet Daniel was more of a go-getter and he was unstoppable in the line of attack. What, by comparison, was he doing wrong?

Stanley, although sensitive, was seldom ponderous; thinking too seriously caused him to panic and abandon all thoughts. *This was something to worry about*, he thought, but he decided to stop the thinking about it for the moment as he ambled along languidly in the play.

Another thing that kept popping up in his head was a phrase out of a recent *Nigerian Daily Observer*: "The bones before the meat and the dressing!" Maybe he had not yet put together the bones or substance of his quest for soccer glory, and he was busy chasing after the meat, dressing, or style, as a sensitive nature rife with imagination and fantasy made him prone to do.

Thinking on this and the rest of what he read in that daily eventually gave him pause, and he shelved all such thinking.

What he read concerned issues of life in general and education in particular. A veteran educationist wrote an article that stated whatever was thought in secondary schools became obsolete by the time students passed out of school, and that students were ill equipped for their onward journey in the real world.

Hence, this veteran educationist called for reform engendered in his plea and theme: the need to give the students the bare bones and facts of life (the real substance) and what they most certainly needed to survive, rather than the meat and dressing (the embellishments or style). After all, according to this veteran's viewpoint, education is a preparation for life and should teach about survival, first and foremost—especially, survival in a rapidly changing world.

For Stanley, this one thing was certain. He knew he owed his parents, despite their recent demise, an eternal debt of gratitude, in that they prepared him and they chose for him to attend Government College. He was therefore wary of any viewpoints, whether or not held by expert educationists, which tended to diminish from how he felt in this matter towards his deceased parents. No person could pass critical judgement on his parents, school or friends. It was a mark of the strong African streak in him. His reasoning and thoughts easily withered whenever they dwelt on very touchy subjects.

Now a ray of hope played on his mind. *What would happen if he were to score a goal in this match?* he fantasized gleefully. Of course, it would gladden his heart. People might stop calling him nicknames like comic footballer. *But, what would it actually take for him to score a goal?* he considered. Now he wasn't sure. *Sheer drive!* he reflected. *Sheer drive! Bare bones! Sheer drive! Bare bones!* he repeated this ditty to himself, with a quiet resolve to aim at scoring a goal.

CHAPTER 6

Christopher Nomo never strayed far from where the school principal, Mr. John Austin, sat on the pavilion. He kept close observation of the school principal and his binoculars. So much, he preferred to miss watching the soccer match itself and expose himself to be sent on further errands.

Christopher's life thus far at Government College ran the gamut in the book *Tom Brown's School Days*. From when, as a "fag," his tail was cut (the class-one students were considered "fags" by the class-two students who obliged themselves in cutting the tails of the class-one students by bringing down the blade of the right palm heavily against the latter's rear end in a painful, swift cutting motion); "initiation" into the school or "baptism," the equivalent of drinking a solution of brine; and the multitudes of errands since then, his healthy constitution, stood him in good stead.

It was through playfulness he coped, and seeming nonchalance. Some of his unwary peers and senior students thought he had become inured. It was an assessment that was far from the truth. In reality, Christopher detested all those errands and the fuss that went with doing them. He longed to break free: get out of being the bottom man on the totem pole. And that, for him, meant to pass his promotion exams into class two and earn himself a fief, as class-two students were so graciously entitled to.

Whereas the class-one students had the most menial of the dormitory or housework, namely, picking up dirt around the dormitory block and cleaning the lavatories, the class-two students had more of the creative portions of housework, such as gardening—sweeping, weeding, and cleaning around the flower beds, and fashioning new flower beds.

As a sidekick, the class-two students would bully the class-one students. Many a time, class-one students would cry out from such "dehumanizing" drills or ill treatment from the class-two students. On a few occasions, a class-two student who unwittingly tried to bully a big class-one student would find out to his shame and hurt that such a big class-one student, who was not intimidated, would react by beating up on the class-two student. Such humiliation would sometimes make a class-two student, along with other fellow class-two students, gang up against a big class-one student. Other times, a no-win situation arose as the big class-one student would subsequently take his complaints to a senior prefect or the house master. The latter was sure to deal with the gang of class-two students. Those were the days long before the emergence of student cults in public school campuses of both secondary and tertiary institutions.

In the dormitories, class-two students had their beds made by class-one students. The class-one students were also sent on innumerable errands by all their seniors, especially by class-two students. Some of such errands included asking the class-one student to go and tell a particular senior student that he was stupid. This was sure to excite the wrath of the senior student to whom a class-one student was sent to call him stupid. It was the lot of the class-one boy, however, to suffer the displaced anger from that senior student. The class-one student, by going on such an errand, was made to act the idiot's script and to play into the hands of both senior students, whose double wrath whipped him silly. More importantly, it made the poor lad a parody of Pilate's declaration to the Sanhedrin in the hall of judgement, *Ecce stupid!*

In the dining hall, the class-one students would normally set the tables and fetch drinking water in jugs from the taps in the scullery. The classes two, three, and four students were then responsible for dishing out the food on plates. Finally, the class-one students had the enviable role of passing the plates of food to each individual student's sitting position around the dining table. This was one of the few assigned roles that class-one students exploited to their own advantage: securing for themselves and their favourite senior students, on some occasions, the most bountiful plate of food. This was an act students nicknamed "construction," a derogatory reference to a class-one boy's sharp crisscrossing of the arms, as his brain, at the same time, went into scheming overdrive just for the sole purpose of "heisting" the targeted bounteous plate of food for himself, and perhaps, the next best plate of food for a favourite senior student. Construction, though frowned upon, was nevertheless a way of life with some students.

As the school principal in rasp attention listened to Gerald, there was a moment of anxiety for Christopher. It was when John Austin's right hand, waving the binoculars, almost smashed them against the concrete post of the railing in front, on the top floor of the pavilion. Christopher started, shifted and lurched forward as if to prevent the possible disaster. It was this movement that attracted the senior boy sitting next to him.

"Class One, would you stop pavilion soccer?" the senior boy cautioned Christopher querulously, in reference to the involuntary kicks or movement of the legs made by some spectators as they got so engrossed in the soccer game out in the field below.

"Yes, please," Christopher answered inaudibly.

"What, by the way, are you doing here? Go and sit with your mates on the field."

Christopher did not answer the senior boy, but on his face played a deliberate vacuous smile, which the senior boy found defiant and very irritating.

The senior boy threatened Christopher loudly and deviously, "How dare you smile at me?"

The history master, not far from the senior boy, felt disturbed by the latter's near monologue and loud outburst. He turned around in his usual painstaking, fiendish manner and snarled at the senior boy.

"Riff raff," he drawled. "Out, out of here you silly thing!" the history master spoke with scarcely concealed contempt, motioning with his right forefinger at the senior boy.

Christopher looked askance, as though he was not involved with the senior boy. Inwardly, however, he felt a satisfied *Schadenfreude* that kind of said "up yours!" in mute defiance to the petulant senior boy. The feeling was short-lived.

CHAPTER 7

A soccer maestro like Pele is said to be incredibly well attuned to every point of play in the game, like a spider at the centre of its own web, this being the main reason such a master player succeeded so well. At the height of perfection, players like that seemingly managed to be everywhere on the field of play, at the same time.

With prodigious fitness, players like that kept the ball throughout the game in the position they played, judging excellently by their keen, total involvement in the play and understanding of the dynamics of the ball. Given, also, that in every well-composed team there are only a few movers and shakers who made things happen, and they, without a doubt, knew themselves that they belonged in that small coterie of fine players.

Daniel Oke tended towards the finesse of a maestro. He knew his own limitations and strengths as well as those of other top players. Just before the halftime, a pass from deep within the Warri House side of the field brought the ball to him somewhere close to the opponent's goal. He tipped forward with it only to be met by the stud-like figure of one Warri House fullback. Oke pulled back with panache, leaving the defender transfixed. He already glimpsed, from the corner of his left eye, Stanley Osa moving into position. A rare combination!

Daniel, on his part, realized he would have to do more work to beat the fullback, and quite possibly he could lose control of the ball if he attempted to score a goal by shooting directly into the net. *Better to pass the ball to Stanley and take the chance that Stanley might score a goal*, he quickly decided.

P-o-o-m! The football sounded, as Daniel's pass brought it to Stanley, who instantly recognized he was free and facing the

16

goal, with the goalkeeper the only obstacle to beat. *Be calm*! he admonished himself. *Or else you'll shoot wild*!

Looking toward the extreme left side of the goalkeeper, Stanley levelled the ball precisely in the opposite flank of the goal. The goalkeeper flipped like an oblong yo-yo. The ball grazed the goalkeeper's outstretched hands while entering the net.

And then, the agony of defeat set in for the goalkeeper. He was still sliding on the grass when he hit the ground in his attempt to prevent the goal. He curled himself into the safe position too late. His head struck the goalpost, and he fainted immediately. Simultaneously, a thunderous cheer rose from the field, not even dampened by any murmur of sympathy for the fallen goalkeeper.

Christopher hurried to the balcony railing, when through the loud cheer he heard someone shout exuberantly, "Comic footballer, up you!"

What did my cousin have to do with the latest goal? Christopher wondered. Just then the whistle blew to mark the halftime recess.

Gazing out to the far side of the field, Christopher spotted Stanley. His cousin was all over Daniel in a bear-hug. It puzzled Christopher, but then, he thought to himself, *Perhaps my cousin scored this last goal with a little teamwork and support from Daniel.*

People talked excitedly on the pavilion. On the field below, a group of first aid workers frantically tried to resuscitate the Warri House goalkeeper. Christopher sifted some of the words that entered his large ears.

"At last, Stanley scored his first major career goal!" said the history master. No one knew how he kept his records, but he did, on virtually everything on campus: students' academic performance, extracurricular activities, breaking of bounds, or more. And like Somerset Maugham's *The Man Who Knew It All*, he would often announce his findings openly, and to no one in particular.

Christopher, on hearing the history master's words from where he stood by the railing, bounded toward the nearer stairway to go down to the field below. Halfway down, he glimpsed the familiar figure of the senior boy who was sent out of the pavilion earlier by the history master.

The senior boy was somewhat lurking by the stairs. He had not yet seen Christopher, who now retreated up the stairs again.

Christopher went to the far end of the pavilion and came down the other stairway. He soon entered the field and after running a short distance, embraced Stanley.

A scene as enigmatic as Degas's *Bonsoir Monsieur Le Duc* soon played itself out. Stanley shifted self-consciously out of Christopher's embrace, but said, "Thank you, Bon-boy."

CHAPTER 8

The sentry by the main gate of Government College knew something was wrong when some local policemen stalked up to his guard house. The time was 5:10 p.m. Intermittent noise was still coming out of the soccer field, so he couldn't imagine there was anything wrong at the field. Riots and hooliganism were practically unheard of at Government College. He wondered, however, why there was a longer-than-usual halftime recess today, the last fifteen minutes when he had not heard any noise from the direction of the soccer field.

"We came to see the principal. Where –" The sergeant with the scar on the bridge of his nose, who led the group of five other policemen, was interrupted. As he spoke, though, the scar appeared to elongate, giving him a false mien.

"I have instructions to not let anyone inside college premises without authorisation," said the sentry in a singsong that interrupted the sergeant's earlier statements.

"But he sent for us. Okay, we will go back!"

"No, don't go back. Allow me to confirm –" It was the sentry's turn to be cut short by the now irate sergeant.

"We will go back and you won't see us here again—o!" the sergeant threatened. "Wait, I will see who I can send with you . . ."

". . . To take you to his quarters." The sentry ended what he was saying, and it seemed to pacify the sergeant and his men.

The minutes ticked by rather slowly, and Bede Olo realized it with anguish. Seated alone on a chair inside a spare room in the principal's boy's quarters, he longed to be told why he was being isolated.

Impulsive as ever, he questioned whoever chanced to pass in front of the open door of the room. He usually got no answers back. He would have come out of the room if not for the events of the last forty minutes, which brought about an unusual, tranquil change in him. It was probably better, he decided, to sit and do as he was told.

Now he considered for the umpteenth time what happened to him in the last forty minutes or so. He remembered falling asleep back at his dormitory and being woken up to the wild stares of three school prefects. Sleeping during games was an infraction, but none too serious as to warrant three prefects being sent to apprehend him. So what was this all about?

The answer was laid out on the faces of the three prefects. In a relay, their faces puckered and relaxed alternately, like they were drawn by strings. Strange marionettes they were, staring down at him, with apprehension written over their faces. The prefect in the middle was visibly shaken and stood back a little.

Silently, deliberately, Bede slowly sat up on his bed. "What have I done?" he asked in flawless English, if only with a voice that was a bit drawn.

That was hardly what the prefects expected to hear. The prefect in the middle could not restrain himself. "Who are you? I mean, you are not a student. Not one of us in this house. So why are you sleeping inside here?" he asked.

"Are you joking? I am Bede Olo."

One of the prefects noted Bede's crisp sentences, especially the annoying stance he used when he uttered them, only his voice was drawn. Even the appearance was vaguely like Bede's, except the body was very gaunt. Perhaps it was the boy's sick father at home who had changed places with him. "But why? How can . . . ?" The prefect could not conjecture.

"How can you convince us? We are looking at a sixty-year-old man who says he's the fourteen-year-old boy we once knew."

"Where's my mirror?" Bede asked in genuine frustration. He retrieved a key from under his pillow and opened his bedside locker to take out a mirror.

One of the prefects noted how he seemed to feel at home opening the locker, only his movements were quite slow.

In his haste to take out the mirror, Bede knocked down a tin container with a loose lid from the locker's top shelf. Three spiders, one big and black, spilled onto the floor and crawled away from the locker. The prefect that stood in the middle drew back a little, but the other two took flight.

"Steer clear of the big black spider," Bede admonished the prefect who tarried by him. "I haven't taken out its sting yet."

The prefect he spoke to paced backwards and inwardly shuddered. The other two, by now, looked on forlornly from the door.

Bede perfunctorily glimpsed his own image before throwing down the mirror on the bed in the aftermath of the spilt spiders. Of course, in the mirror he had seen his same robust self, with thick black eyelids, the eyes themselves, those of a sage, wary of confronting his own awesome identity. Why did everyone say he had changed? He felt peculiar ire as he reflected. Then he calmly replaced each spider in the container and put the lid back on.

"Can't you see you are not Bede?" the prefect who stood by asked plaintively.

"Let's go and see the principal," one of the other two prefects spoke jerkily, as the two of them joined the third prefect close to Bede's bedside.

He quietly followed them to the soccer field where the principal was watching the soccer match.

Afterwards, the principal, bemused by the whole story and circumstance of it, instructed that Bede be brought to this room in the principal's boy's quarters where he now sat.

John Austin, principal of Government College, seldom assumed a serious stance. He was conscious of the strain it produced on him, and his skin suffered ticks. Besides, after losing a wife and his only son, he was convinced that nothing should again stress him.

His personal conviction was, however, falling apart right this moment in the face of an improbable situation. It was what Gerald, the head of school, had come to discuss with him a while ago on the pavilion.

"Incredible! Capital!" Austin exasperated. To think a boy of fourteen years left sleeping in his dormitory at the onset of the football match could, in less than thirty minutes, be transformed into a rickety old man of sixty. How could anyone believe that? More importantly, how would he, John Austin, resolve the situation? The boy's parents would at any moment now be breathing down his neck, seeking redress and threatening all out war.

John Austin suddenly remembered a German phrase, *Der Hergott würfelt nicht*, credited to the late scientist Albert Einstein, the translation of which embodied the scientist's lifelong belief that God does not play dice with human life. That is to say, God does not practice "trial and error" where human destiny was concerned; hence, the ultimate laws of nature were free from caprice. John wished he could believe that. Right now he felt sure Providence was playing a pun on him. How else could he explain this seemingly unexplainable and unexpected event at a time when he looked forward to a quiet retirement? He had run this school without incidence for four years. Why now should the end of the rainbow shift from everything real, everything sedate and familiar . . . and unto something quite weird?

He resolved not to be daunted. Already a stratagem for coping with this unforeseen situation was forming in his big strong head. He wished he himself had the detective skills of Sherlock Holmes, but what good would they do in such a setting? Sherlock Holmes never solved any real African mysteries. But seriously, he considered sending for help from Scotland Yard. He would have to communicate with the British Consul in Lagos and discuss the matter with him.

CHAPTER 9

John Austin returned to his quarters before the soccer match ended. The scores then were School House 2, Warri House 0. He imagined the match would end on those scores; the two teams looked spent. Now he would turn his attention to the more pertinent matter of the boy turned old man.

He drove home in two minutes. His 1965 model Mercedes Benz was still going strong, like the decanter of Johnnie Walker that regularly graced his bar shelf at home. He took with him the head of school and the arts master.

Just before he turned from the Appian Way into Principal's Drive—the street he alone lived on—a frantic wave straight ahead by the school's main gate caught his eye. John Austin was obliged to let off the arts master to find out what that was all about. The arts master came down from the car and strode straight to the gate.

On getting to his quarters, John Austin saw six policemen lolling around his front porch. They immediately stood erect when his car entered the driveway. Obsequious grins played on their faces as he stood out of the car.

"Come round to the back of the house," said the head of school to the policemen, voicing out the unspoken thoughts of Mr. John Austin.

The scar on the leading policeman's face danced nervously.

"Wetin *oyibo* man call us for now?" He grumbled to his colleagues in pigeon English, while they still wore their sheepish grins.

With the utmost care, like one handling incendiary, the head of school shepherded the policemen to the back of the house. He soon brought them to the spare room in the boy's quarters, where Bede Olo was being isolated. Afterwards, he told the policemen the principal's request. The boy, no man, was to be watched constantly for the next few days until some decisive steps could be taken on his matter. He did not expatiate on any of the things he told the policemen; it was as the principal desired.

The policemen were unimpressed. The sergeant with the scar grumbled loudly. It stood to reason: the lot of policemen was doing dog work, or what sort of work it was this time he couldn't be certain. However, he was sure the principal would see his boss, the DPO, later to show his appreciation. He grumbled again before his beady eyes took in the whole scene around him.

He was not in the least bit interested in their assignment. The old man they were to watch couldn't possibly give them any trouble, so naturally his mind turned to other matters. He noticed the head of school's polite stance as the latter tarried, after informing them of their assignment, and he ventured a question.

"How do we get food and drink?"

"You will be served food and water at our dining hall. You will have to form two groups, so one group can keep watch while the other group is eating."

The head of school was soon summoned by the principal, after he answered the lead policeman's question.

Bede could not believe his ears. *I, Bede, am to be watched; for what? Sleeping during a football match? My parents must hear of this! I can't stand it anymore.*

Yet thoughts of his parents brought an imperceptible change in him. It was as though he was severed from them. Besides, an independent spirit like him sought no anchors. Such were provided naturally, by providence, more than they could be sought. He relented in his thinking, and resolved to let events carry him from day to day and for as long as they could. Even a cavalier attitude can brook no ill will, unless tempered by seriousness, or call it faith. Ill will for Bede was anything that impugned his carefree attitude and existence, which being constantly watched by the police, of all people, amounted to. There was inner strength he drew from, which he never knew he had. Soon he would get used to his new situation. He fielded the consort of six policemen with jokes, tottering at first, like a fledgling. They spurned him, but he was undaunted.

"What's the matter with you officers?" he fumed after a particularly unfruitful spell. "Can't you take a joke? Or is it that I have become your Caesar's tribute?"

The policemen laughed pitifully at him, but began to call him *Caesar's tribute* or simply *Caesar*, in mockery both of what he said and of his current helpless state.

CHAPTER 10

John Austin was pacing up and down in his living room when the head of school entered. The principal's secretary, notepad and pencil in hand, looked like he had the sword of Damocles hanging over him. He dared not look up from his notepad. Somehow, the presence of another black person in the living room, especially the head of school, gave him assurance.

Only weeks old in his new job, John Austin's secretary never had to listen to a foreigner before. He found his boss's accent strange, his speech swift, the words staccato and their nuance daunting, making him want to abandon listening to him and to take flight.

Curiously, his understanding of his boss's speech improved when he least seemed perturbed, especially now that no less a person as the head of school was present. Now he relaxed in his note taking, and strange words fell in line after line on his notepad; their purpose eternally lucid.

> *11 June*
> *Dear Douglas (Principal Designate),*
> *I am obliged to send for you, on account of a strange occurrence at the college today. It is too soon to know what to make of it; whether or not a school boy actually changed to an old man as it is believed.*
> *However, I would need your presence, cooperation and support in resolving this mystery. Besides, I believe it would be of benefit for you to have an insight into whatever happens at the college from now on.*
> *With utmost regards,*
> *John Austin*

The head of school maintained unobtrusive presence until the principal finished dictating his second letter. John Austin now addressed him.

"I want liveliness around the school. Let the dormitories maintain their usual regimen of Saturday entertainment. I don't want it looking like there's a pall hanging over everyone!"

"Sure, sir," the head of school said curtly in a manner of welcome agreement, which at the same time conveyed to the principal that he made a foresighted decision, and he, the head of school, could be trusted to carry it out absolutely.

John Austin promptly dismissed the head of school and afterwards returned to dictating. His next letter was to the British Consul, and he dictated it rather self-consciously.

> *11 June*
>
> *I've got to tell you, this is not regular fare! A mystery or some such that quite requires, in my humble opinion, the detective skills of Sherlock Holmes has occurred. A school boy of fourteen has inexplicably changed into an old man of sixty. And that is why I am imploring you to quickly send for a detective from Scotland Yard. No doubt, Her Majesty's Service would benefit immensely from the experience of resolving this mystery.*
>
> *John Austin.*

CHAPTER 11

The head of school fleeted through Principal's Drive jauntily until he reached the T-junction with the Appian Way. Then he fell into his usual sedate, yet rippling gait, like he was the messenger of God. His big eyes flashed right and then left and then right again. He had an appropriate message, but it had to wait for the moment.

A final din from the direction of the soccer field tempted to hasten him. A thousand thoughts jammed in his mind, each wanting instant resolution. He gave his mind pause and took matters afresh from when the principal declared what amounted to a glorious Saturday entertainment day.

Nothing could be more quintessential than asking a school yard of overwrought kids to have some fun. He was sure they would enjoy doing so, after the soccer match and the day's uncanny incident of the changed boy. Thinking of the soccer match and the other incident, he felt hurried again for a short time only before he settled into his lonely contemplation. The head of school had his personal desires to somehow, someday organise a massive treasure hunt game, one involving the entire school. He needed no clairvoyant to tell him that now was his chance.

Any house (or dormitory block) that did not have a special recreational activity planned for the night would be co-opted into the treasure hunt game by him. Names of heads of house (or senior dormitory prefects) who would assist him in writing clues were already coming up in his mind. He and two other fellow prefects would evaluate the acceptability of clues, and he alone would place all the clues. He would ensure there was no form of chicanery in this rare treasure hunt game.

His thought of a unique treasure hunt triggered his mind again. What would the student population achieve by this massive treasure hunt game? Like in all creative work, he felt prescience was required here. Why not toss that question to the triumvirate, who would endorse written clues, to resolve? Deep within himself, he knew what he wanted to achieve. To ginger every student's creative spirit even in such a playful setting, or sort of have a "third eye" on things, to borrow an idiom from the title of Tibetan writer Lobsam Rampa's book.

And talking about creativity, he knew one of a few things about the subject, like the necessity of letting go or having the mind run free. Call it imagination or something like that, but it's also letting go the reins so the mind could range far and wide over unfamiliar terrain. In doing so, intuition came to the forefront.

As most ideas crystallized, which the head of school had for the treasure hunt, he ambled down the rest of the Appian Way at a leisurely pace. He went directly to his dormitory, School House.

The first of the students trickled in from the soccer field. The head of school quickly summoned a form-three student to his corner in one of the fingers of the n-shaped building.

"Up School House!" The cry from some students newly returned from the soccer field filled the air. Meanwhile, the form-three boy darted his gaze here and there, as he waited for the head of school, who was writing a note. The note was to be circulated to all the heads of house (or senior house prefects) and it read as follows:

> *11/6*
> *To All Heads of House,*
> *Please meet me post-haste, to deliberate on a joint treasure hunt recreation for this night.*
> *Regards,*
> *G. Egbe*

The form-three student was to pass it round to the senior house prefects in all the six other dormitories, namely Forcados, Warri, Sapele, Ashaka, Oleh and Orerokpe Houses.

It was about 6.00 p.m. by now. The head of school realized he had about fifteen minutes before and after dinner to arrange everything for the treasure hunt. It was a tight schedule; however, he expected a speedy response to the summons conveyed by his note.

CHAPTER 12

Warri House was the first port of call for the form-three student bearing the head of school's note. All the dormitories were identical, and each was shaped in a square, but downturned "U" form. Where the two longitudinal fingers joined the transverse web, were two parallel, arched and open thresholds. The four open arched thresholds at the ends of the long corridor, running along the transverse web of each dormitory, provided a short and ready access when going from dormitory to dormitory. The transverse web was longer by twice the breath of each longitudinal dormitory and comprised of two small dormitories (including one formerly called the Common Room), one on either side of the centralized prep hall. Lastly, there was a lavatory at each end of the transverse web.

Each dormitory and the prep hall had a door that could be locked, although these were seldom locked. Each lavatory had a screen wall beyond its open threshold, so the shower area was not visible from the corridor, which ran the entire length of the transverse web. Neither were the three water closets, each with a door visible from the corridor. The floor of the corridor was sunken, except between the arched thresholds at both ends of the transverse web.

Depending on how clean a lavatory was—Warri House's was not particularly neat—one hastened through the outermost arched threshold, either to escape the perennial foul smells emanating from adjacent water closets, or else to avoid the stinking open drain that carried waste water from the hand basins and urinals to a septic tank at the back of the lavatory. The degree of odium surrounding the outermost arched open threshold testified to whether or not the adjacent lavatory was used by senior or by junior boys. A lesser degree of smell resulted when a lavatory was used by senior boys and vice versa, when a lavatory was used by junior boys.

At the outermost open threshold leading into Warri House from School House, the form three-student dropped the head of school's note, through a fitful wave of his left hand holding the note. The note fell right into the open drain nearby. He hastened to retrieve it, but when he found the paper was now somewhat soaked in the putrid water he hesitated.

Just then the head of Warri House, whom he meant to give the note to, dashed out of the open threshold nearby. The form-three boy turned around momentarily to see in which direction the senior prefect was heading. The head of Warri House made a beeline away from both School and Warri Houses. He could probably be going as far as the school's main gate, depending on what duty called for at this time of the evening.

"Excuse me, please!" the form-three student called out to the senior house prefect. "I have a message for you from the head of school."

"What's it about?" The head of Warri House turned to ask, unenthused.

"I believe it is urgent, and it concerns . . ." the form-three student stopped mid-sentence, as he simultaneously wheeled round and squatted by the open drain. Poking his left hand daintily in the gutter, he retrieved the note.

Meanwhile, the impatient senior house prefect spoke up, exasperated. "Answer me. What is it about?"

"It's written here. It's written here." The form-three boy gave the prefect the partially soaked note.

The senior prefect frowned as he joined the form-three boy. "One can never rely on any of you to give messages properly. Now you're handing me a soaked note."

The form-three boy winced but kept quiet.

"What? A treasure hunt? It's late. Anyhow, see Ringin, the duty prefect. He's in the Common Room." the head of Warri House blurted out. He handed the soaked note back to the form-three boy and was gone like a phantom.

The form-three boy crossed the open threshold, and instantly merged with the flow of busy students. Some of those students were returning from the soccer field, with many of them scurrying all around as they tried to take their showers in readiness to go to the dining hall.

He hurried along with the note. Soon he found the diminutive Ringin to whom he gave the note, telling him the head of Warri House asked him to give it to him, and that he should respond on the head of Warri House's behalf.

"Is that really so?" Ringin questioned the form-three boy, after the latter stated his mission.

"So, you have given me the note . . ." Ringin now said, trying to annoy the form-three boy, who all this while politely looked on waiting for him to give back the note, and perhaps indicate a response. "Oh, you want the note back, huh? Here, you can have it."

The form-three student waited a little longer, just to ascertain his commitment towards the note. Ringin glared and drew his now contorted face close, staring straight into the form-three boy's eyes. The latter turned around, but didn't cower, and continued on the rest of his errand.

CHAPTER 13

What a chore to have anything to do with imbeciles! the form-three boy fumed to himself as he left Ringin. *But they are not the worst people on earth*, he thought deeply to himself now, as if he doubted the sense of his silent, exasperating comment.

In reality, the form-three student now churned over a few deep-seated thoughts apparently triggered by his encounter with Ringin. He was the type of person who questioned himself relentlessly in order to make sense of most things happening around him. He couldn't see anything he did wrong to warrant such nasty behaviour from Ringin.

What point was there in doing things right? he questioned in silent indignation. *And having insults for compliments?*

The form-three boy soon reached the head of Forcados House with the note. The latter's reply was most blatant, "Who does that obsequious fool think he is, sending me a note like this? Tell him to get lost!" Staring hard at the suddenly self-conscious, form-three boy, he finally said, "And you can do likewise!"

The form-three boy instantly bristled and eyed the senior prefect with an abstracted look. *No doubt,* he thought to himself, *this is the utterance of an irresponsible senior student who ought not to have been made a prefect anyway.* Afterwards, the form-three student withdrew.

It was getting somehow late, when he swung round in the opposite direction to give the same note to the heads of Sapele, Ashaka, Oleh and Orerokpe Houses.

"I must remember to tell the head of school what the head of Forcados House said," the form-three boy grumbled to himself. And then he calmly moved along to the next contact.

The response from the head of Sapele House was out rightly favourable. "That's fine. I need to see him anyway, regarding something else," the spindly senior house prefect spoke in a heart-warming stance.

As they say in GCU, the index or pointer of geniality turns from the left to the right along the horseshoe (or crescent) line of dormitory buildings. To the left (facing due north) are the hot-heads; and to the right, their antipodes—the fellows with natural bonhomie. Going on to Ashaka House, the form-three student soon confirmed this adage.

The head of Ashaka House was meeting with the house master at the latter's staff quarters round the back of the dormitory, so the form-three boy waited a while before he could see this senior house prefect. After he met him, the huge bespectacled senior house prefect read the note and smiled.

"Sure. In fact, we in Ashaka House had a treasure hunt game planned for the night. I guess this note has changed all that now," he said indulgently.

The form-three student couldn't help feeling self-satisfied as he went on his way to Oleh House. *The head of Ashaka House sure has personal charm*, he reflected, *and strength of character too*. In this latter attribute he was next probably only to the head of school, as many students had often said among themselves. There was also that air of insouciance about him, besides his pleasantness. The form-three boy, if only he knew the right words, would have said that the head of Ashaka House looked the better part of a first generation African statesman or diplomat, the likes of Leopold Senghor of Senegal or Zik of Africa.

The head of Oleh House, to whom the form-three student gave the head of school's note next, was a squat fellow with a chiselled face, incessantly bothered at having to look authoritative or to stare at other students, especially his juniors, who were taller than himself. His face twitched repeatedly after he read the note and began to say something.

"I will like to write the clues. But who's going to participate in the treasure hunt if there's a student demonstration tonight?"

he asked rhetorically. His face twitched again. "Well, I'm on my way."

The head of Orerokpe House was away from the school leading a team of drama students to a national competition in Lagos, so the form-three boy with the note was informed. The house prefect on duty initially refrained from accepting any responsibility in connection with the note. In earnest, this Orerokpe House duty prefect was looking forward to an idle Saturday night, one he would spend in the corner of his dormitory perusing blue books, while the usual Saturday entertainment or dance party took place under supervision of his nominated senior student. The note, however, changed all that. He went on his way grudgingly to meet with the head of school, but never really got to him.

CHAPTER 14

His first career goal just behind him, Stanley Osa was doing his best to look a demigod as he strode from the soccer field to the dormitory. Suddenly, it seemed everything was well within his forte. And as happens in such self-conscious reflections, he expected everyone else around to appreciate this change in him and to doff. Some students around probably would have done so, given his own lacklustre antecedents, but they were too absorbed in the disquieting transformation of Bede Olo. Overall, many of the students talked of the incident in small groups and in hushed tones. A vocal minority group of students, however, talked of the matter in harsh words, threatening fire and brimstone against the school authorities for the latter's perceived poor handling of the matter.

In spite of his latest self-awareness, Stanley found the news of the incident disquieting, although he did not personally know the student called Bede Olo. He, however, suppressed the disquieting thought, which then released a new sensation like a high-blown spirit, fluttering mostly and settling in a whirlwind. Stanley settled on the flowery interlude of the most recent exciting experience in his life: the goal he scored at the soccer match that day.

As his thoughts went in a circle around the goal and himself, Stanley began to affect the mannerisms of Homer's "uncompanionable" fellow. *From now on I must make it my business to excel always in everything I do*, he told himself.

How nice, he thought again, to the accompaniment of his own majestic steps. *If only I could do just that. Of course, I would have to put my mind into everything I do, one hundred percent, and that would be saying it mildly.* A quote then intruded somewhere in his mind: *"In war, there is no second prize for runner up,"* though he couldn't recall who made that statement. Anyhow, that did not matter. Perhaps all that mattered was that he himself would have to treat every endeavour like war. That was perfectly okay; a small prize to be paid for what he wanted.

"Is that so?" Stanley now queried, in an affected guttural voice, everything others said to him. Not for want of understanding, but because his thoughts dared not stray from the only conscious point and true centre of the universe—himself. Whenever he uttered the query, he would stomp on the ground as if with the sole purpose of shaking the earth loose and pressing his own footprints into it for all times.

Along the way, he threw his strides carelessly forward and inadvertently stepped on the heels of another fellow player in the soccer match just ended that day. The pain was shared by the two of them, but the other player turned around, infuriated.

"Why did you mash me, comic footballer?" the other player questioned, waiting for a chance to inflict pain on Stanley also.

"Is that so?" Stanley now asked in his newly adopted manner, more out of abstraction than any sense of remorse. The other player stared menacingly at him, and before Stanley had time to think of a better response or apologize, the irate fellow player stepped back on his foot and ran wildly.

Stanley pursued him hot foot, seeking retribution. Winded too soon, though, he fell back in step with another group of students walking twenty yards ahead of where he stepped on the other fellow player's heels. The other fellow player now got away, like a nettled rabbit.

As he regained his breath, Stanley sifted some of the conversation going on within the new group of students, in the midst of whom he was walking. He realized immediately that they were talking about the mysterious change that happened to Bede Olo.

A notorious form-five student in the group, an expert in inciting students towards taking up the cudgel and in most other clandestine activities, now spoke up vehemently, "Is this how they're going to handle this matter? Before you know it, we will all age prematurely."

Stanley decided to ignore this group of students; in fact, he maintained his own studious silence until he heard the same form-five student speak again. After giving Stanley, a significant glance, the form-five student began threatening a demonstration.

"Bite your tongue!" Stanley almost quipped out loud, while he looked on the form-five boy as one who committed an unforgiveable act. As Stanley knew very well, this form-five student was a ferret of some sort, known for his flair in bringing out the worst attributes from the students. Left unchecked, this form-five student could mastermind a demonstration. To Stanley, however, the seriousness with which that student spoke of a demonstration seemed out of proportion to, or incongruous with, the sudden mysterious aging of their fellow schoolmate. Something certainly had to be done. And in all probability, something was already being done at the appropriate quarters, i.e. by the school authorities. Stanley couldn't see any role, least of all a demonstration, for the generality of students in this critical matter. He decided that he would apprise the head of school of the threat by that form-five student.

Near the end of the concourse of four soccer fields, the group of students, including the provocative form-five student, veered to the left and entered a footpath that would take each student to his respective dormitory.

Stanley was left alone keeping a straight course for his dormitory, School House. His big head inched upward slowly on his shoulders, and feeling slightly more relaxed now, he walked almost erect.

CHAPTER 15

Just past the dining hall and before he too would veer off to the right to enter his dormitory premises, Stanley was met by his excited young cousin, Chris Nomo.

"Bon-boy, how are you?" Stanley asked felicitously, while at the same time, his rickety legs became suddenly pronounced.

Everyone in their families called the young lad Bon-boy. A few people often thought that Bon-boy had quirks of character that easily translated into unpredictable behaviour. While others said that it was merely a form of youthful exuberance that maturity would, in time, take away. Stanley often had his own misgivings about this fellow, but he felt it was because of his impulsiveness due perhaps to his immaturity.

Initial pleasantries aside, Bon-boy now seemed withdrawn. Standing beside Stanley, he looked like he was seeking acceptance from the somewhat tall and strapping cousin of his before uttering any words.

Stanley, never ever apologetic and not one to be goaded with such stance of unspoken thoughts, initially looked on forlornly. He soon tired of waiting, however, and spoke to the young lad, "Maybe you should see me in my dormitory after dinner."

He noticed that Christopher Nomo did not move, but managed a half smile back, and opened his big mouth. "You want to tell me something?"

"Yes. I was in a terrible dream last night . . ." the young lad began.

Stanley shifted and frowned, for Christopher was looking intensely at him as he spoke.

This thought kept recurring to Stanley, *Persistently giving with one hand and taking away with the other spoils conversa-*

tion. Then suddenly from nowhere, this clerihew blazed through his mind:

> *The moustache of Adolf Hitler*
> *Could hardly be littler,*
> *Was the thought that kept recurring*
> *To Field Marshal Goering*

The quotation and the clerihew were like balm that soothed Stanley well under the circumstances, preventing his large oval face from breaking into full-blown hostility toward the young lad. Against his own impulse, Stanley refrained from withdrawing the earlier invitation to Christopher Nomo to visit him in his dormitory after dinner.

Stanley did not believe in dreams. In fact, he never recalled any dream of his own. All he knew about dreams was what his chemistry tutor told his class—that is, the scientist Kekulé received intuitive knowledge as to the structural formula of the ringed benzene molecule through a dream.

"What was the dream about?" Stanley asked Christopher.

"A big boat, not the Government College ship, was turned by strong winds in the wrong direction. I was coxswain on the boat and I laboured strenuously to turn the boat around in the proper direction. Everyone else on the crew was against me. Somehow, you were present on the boat and instinctively, I turned to you for help. Just then, however, you fell overboard. In horror I raced to the side of the big boat to throw you the lifeline. Several of the other crew members prevented me. One of them shouted, 'Run him over!' and I raced back in agony to the turning wheel to prevent you from being run over in the water by the boat, and possibly to come broadsides close to you in the water. However, the turning wheel was now firmly controlled by the other members of the crew who were against me. I cried out loud, 'Throw me overboard also!' and then I awoke."

Stanley paused for a few seconds before he spoke to Christopher Nomo again.

"I must tell you, I do not believe in dreams. Some people do, I'm sure, and from what I have been told, dreams may be a source of inspiration. But let me ask you this: What do you think is the meaning of this dream?"

"I was hoping you would help me with the interpretation, but I'm sorry you don't believe in dreams. I usually try to interpret it myself, however, I have never dreamt about such a complex situation before."

"Well, I might be able to assist you somehow," Stanley said as he reflected a little. "One of my classmates has a little book about dreams that might help you."

"Would you borrow the book from this classmate of yours for me to read and return?"

"Yes. Yes. This classmate of mine once said to me that according to the book, such phenomena as dreams arose from repressed feelings, especially of guilt, sin or conscience. Anyway, I didn't understand all what he said to me then, and I told him so before leaving that matter where it has stayed between us. But for your sake, since it appears you worry about your dreams, especially this latest one, I will borrow the book for you."

"Thanks, I will see you in your dormitory tonight," Christopher said before he raced toward his dormitory in Ashaka House.

CHAPTER 16

Stanley entered his dormitory inside School House at the same time the form-three boy sent by the head of school returned from giving the senior school prefect's note to all the other senior house prefects.

Most of the other students were at this time set to go to the dining hall and were actually beginning to move out in that direction in small groups. Stanley vacillated between getting himself set for dinner right away and letting the head of school know about the possibility of a demonstration, planned for later that night by some unknown students. He settled on the latter course of action first. Duty, he assured himself, demanded he should inform the head of school promptly on anything possibly disruptive. Duty before dinner!

The chiselled face head of Oleh House was with the head of school when Stanley walked tentatively towards the senior prefect's corner in the long "A" dormitory. The form-three boy who just passed him in the corridor was now with the head of school, giving him a sort of report and handing over a small note to him. Afterwards, the form-three boy left the head of school, and the latter was left with the head of Oleh House.

Chisel Face, as Stanley saw, was every bit the ascetic and erudite senior student he was reputed to be. And now like a stand-up comedian, he proceeded to describe various scenarios concerning a treasure hunt for the head of school's benefit. He went on to itemize clues with evident perspicacity.

"Did you ever get that feeling of déjà vu the first time you walked by the disused old concrete water tank?" Chisel Face asked the senior school prefect.

The Head of School did not immediately answer.

Stanley was wary of interrupting this duo that seemed bent on carrying out some form of intellectual minuet, albeit, on scraps of paper.

"Well, I think we should place a clue there," Chisel Face pressed on. "It's an immense monument, especially now that it is decommissioned."

"Write the lead and the positional clues for it. I trust you can do that. Besides, I think you and I should begin at once to write all the clues required, since the other prefects are not here and we have very little time left. I alone will place the clues accepted for use in this unique treasure hunt game."

"Unique indeed," Chisel Face chuckled as he settled down by a bedside locker to begin writing clues on the notebook he brought with him. First, he cut various sizes of scraps of paper and then he started to write on the first scrap of paper.

"Oh please, I'm sorry to interrupt you, but some unknown students are threatening to demonstrate this night," Stanley now said after waiting a while. "You may wish to investigate the matter."

Chisel Face looked up to say, "Come to think of it I have heard of a similar thing, but it appears so unrealistic that I have not given too much thought to it."

"Thanks for telling me," said the head of school who nodded at the same time toward the head of Oleh House. "Give this note to the prefect on duty to announce when you get to the dining hall."

The senior prefect's note concerned the treasure hunt and it indicated the cadets' parade ground in front of the main school block would be the venue or mustering point for the game. The timing, it pointed out, would be right after dinner.

Stanley left for his dormitory to immediately prepare and get to the dining hall in order to promptly give the head of school's note to the duty prefect.

Holding his pen in his left hand, Chisel Face now hunched over the scraps of paper on the bedside locker. He decided he would write the clues for the old water tank first. He reflected in a cursory manner on what exactly he ought to write as the lead clue for the old relic. *It has to be something quite memorable,* he told himself, *a sort of magnum opus.*

"I stand here now an old, decrepit empty water tank," Chisel Face wrote on his scrap of paper, but crossed out the word "decrepit" afterwards. He told himself the amendment should do for the positional or discovered clue, but the lead or herald clue had to be more telling, possibly even dramatic, so as to stick in the mind of any student that would go out there to hunt for this clue. He looked up at the ceiling, scratched his head with the back of his pen and after a while he began to write on another scrap of paper.

"Gone are the days when I used to be a masterpiece and a sole director of a constituent in life, but now I'm left a mere vacuum. What am I?" Chisel Face finished writing the lead clue for the water tank. He read it to himself, and then he pondered over it quickly.

In what way was it a masterpiece? he asked himself. *Considering it was the first of its type in that part of the country when it was constructed in colonial time, it could pass for a masterpiece,* he thought, and then he moved on to the next clue.

Before continuing, he glanced over at the head of school, whom he now saw was struggling to write his first clue.

"How far have you got writing your first clue?" Chisel Face asked the head of school.

"Not far, but not bad I guess," answered the senior school prefect.

"Let's give ourselves ten minutes for writing all the clues, so we don't drift. That would give you enough time to place the clues before the commencement of the treasure hunt, okay?" Chisel Face proposed.

"You've got it."

The next five minutes went like clockwork. The head of school came up with three pairs of clues while Chisel Face finished writing five pairs of clues. Intermittently they compared the clues. All were acceptable, except one or two that had to be rewritten. Soon they had all ten pairs of clues, which both of them decided were adequate for the game.

CHAPTER 17

It was as they finished writing all the clues that the head of Ashaka House walked in. "Oh, am I late already?"

"I expected you and the other heads of houses to have been here before now, so we could carry out the principal's instructions, but only the head of Oleh House showed up on time. He and I have finished writing the clues for tonight's game of treasure hunt."

"Head of School, let's sanction the other prefects who didn't show up at all," Chisel Face said mischievously.

"Suggest something then."

"Let them buy all the snacks to be consumed at the end of the treasure hunt game."

"Is that enough sanction?"

"Yes, I think so. You can decide on the quantity of snacks."

"Enough for the entire school."

"Can I say something?" the head of Ashaka House now asked.

"Go ahead," replied the head of school.

"A few of the other prefects who are not here may have valid reasons for their absence."

"We will see about that, but they would buy us snacks as their contribution. Now that leaves you out. What would you like to contribute? We are not tasking you."

"I'll join in buying the snacks. I appreciate, of course, it's voluntary on my part."

"It's settled then."

The head of school brought out a torchlight and, tucking the envelope containing the clues and a cello tape under his arm, he proceeded at a fast trot to place all the clues. The other two senior house prefects left to go to the dining hall.

Placing ten clues at various locations scattered randomly within much of the one-mile-square campus was daunting task; however, the head of school had a lion-hearted determination to go through with it. He was buoyed by a feeling of anticipation. A hilarious time certainly awaited the students this night during their participation in the treasure hunt, and that would be to his credit. Naturally, he savoured that expectation with relish. After all, a game like this one could very easily go down in the annals of Government College as one of those extraordinarily rare, creative moments in the life of most students—a once-in-a-lifetime chance.

As the head of school traversed between the higher school (i.e. H.S.C. or sixth form) block and the main school block, his right foot stepped on a small fleshy cushion. He could feel the cushion spring out from under his foot through the rubber slippers he wore. He recoiled his foot instinctively and beamed his torchlight on the spot with such incredible speed. He was in time to see a small startled serpent slitter away into the grass by the roadside. Initially, he swung his right hand as if to stone the serpent as it moved swiftly away; however, he held back his hand.

Was it a good omen? Perhaps it was, the senior prefect reflected. This encounter with the serpent appeared symbolic in a way: the sort of thing the elders would say bespoke of a good outcome for an impending event, say the treasure hunt or even resolving the debacle surrounding the changed Bede Olo.

Thank God the snake did not bite him. After all, not everyone who ever stepped on a serpent walked away unhurt. Now, he hoped that there would be no other serpent warming itself on the coal tar of the streets ahead of where he would tread, or ahead of where the throng of students would trample on this night.

When the head of school got to the old concrete water tank, he let the partially lit scene around this abandoned relic drench him. The tranquil surrounding, accentuated by outside lighting from the nearby and fairly distant staff quarters and school dormitories, each in its own grounds, made him recall the expression "European

Quarters;" a term reserved for the usually well laid-out residences of expatriate personnel, mostly Europeans, with fresh meaning.

Surely this was a well-planned school campus, a school campus that would have been unrivalled in its heyday. Sadly though, this particular object of his quest had no spotlight or any form of external lighting, which made the distant lighting of the surrounding houses to leave it standing in a partial silhouette, against its immediate background. Mark Anthony, the murdered Caesar's friend, would have loved such a scene to do a beautiful oratory about this sorry state of neglect. In his inevitable absence, however, the penmanship of the head of Oleh House would just have to suffice.

With that reflection, the head of school quickly pasted the positional or object clue in a non-too-accessible underside of a beam in the old concrete water tank's support. From there he proceeded to paste the clues meant for the various other facilities or objects dotting the campus: namely, the belfry near the Assembly Hall, the warning stake by the big outfall, the covered walkways to and from the Assembly Hall, the door of the Senior Staff Room, the tennis courts, the school's ship or mascot at the terminal end of the Appian Way, the window framing the statue in the Principal's office, the exit stepping stone of the Higher School Classroom block, and the uncompleted swimming pool.

The head of school trudged around for another fifteen minutes, from one location to the other, until he completed his task. As he approached the dining hall thereafter, he saw that quite a number of the students began to exit the building, and most of them were headed in the direction of the school cadets' parade ground. He hastened inside the dining hall, made an announcement, ate his dinner and hurried ahead of the rest of the students to the cadets' parade ground or cadets' quad.

CHAPTER 18

"Attention, *s'il vous plait*!"

If the Head of School had sounded "bomb alert!" he would not have got as much attention as he did now by prefacing his announcements in strident French remarks, after ringing the bell. The students in the dining hall all became very quiet.

"As you must have been informed, proceed from here to the cadets' parade ground right after your dinner. We want to treat you to a special entertainment tonight. A special recreation called the treasure hunt has been designed to thrill you, especially if you like the excitement of chasing after hidden clues that task both your imagination and ability to solve riddles. We would tell you more about it at the parade ground."

There was a mild shuffling among the students now. The senior prefect paused, and then he continued.

"On a slightly different note, it has come to my notice that most of us treat weekends on campus as times to let loose. But let me warn you; Saturday dance party or entertainment is not a license for violating the school rules and regulation. Worse still, it is unbecoming that some students would insult a prefect when called to order by such a prefect."

A rhythmic hum swept across the dining hall, from one end to the other.

"Remember, as future leaders, we must abide by strict discipline or else none of us can achieve any lasting mark. Therefore, don't be impudent, don't be recalcitrant, and don't be insubordinate."

Excited cheers from the students in the dining hall greeted the senior prefect's concluding remarks. Then he rang the bell again.

"Now let's all quickly join the other students who are already at the cadets' parade ground."

Not long afterwards, the game of treasure hunt commenced. The senior school prefect described the modus operandus before he read out herald clue number one. Each time, he would draw the attention of the students by ringing the bell, and also whenever the noise level became unbearable.

"Gone are the days when I used to be a masterpiece and a sole director of a constituent in life. But now I'm left a mere vacuum. What am I?"

It was amazing how those few lines fell on the students ears. Like a magic wand the words mesmerized and then triggered the students like a mysterious wake-up call. The senior school prefect enjoyed it all, seeing the mass of students come alive again in a very different form now. Seeing it all made up for his thrill, much like witnessing his brainchild become reality and a source of challenge and hilarity. *Too bad*, he told himself, *if anyone would miss out of this unique evening delight*, and then some words of the bard of Avon came to his mind. Before the battle of Agincourt, as Shakespeare had recalled it, King Henry aroused his men from sleep by declaring, "And gentlemen now a' bed in England would think themselves accursed they were not here."

Almost immediately, a large number of student groups formed, and each donned its thinking cap, huddled together and began to brainstorm in low tones. Once the brainstorming session was over, several groups of top sprinters bolted off in the chosen locations, to search out clue number one. Several students bruised themselves in the initial mêlée. Many false starts were inevitable in the run-up to establishing each group's battle readiness, position in the emerging hierarchy and in the final outcome.

Right from the start, a number of students began to play spoilsport, by shouting out spurious search clue locations, especially after locating the first clue. A few students in some groups or houses, swung into action as scouts. This category of students began to pick out search locations from the efforts of other groups that were more successful than their own. Thus a scout would listen attentively to decipher when a clue was found, so as to report the general or precise location to his group members. The competitive spirit was warmly kindled in a smart way by the night's treasure hunt.

CHAPTER 19

A house prefect by the name of Burke organised the Warri House students for a proper participation in the treasure hunt. His goal was that Warri House would win first position in the game.

"Proper preparation," he reminded his house mates, "prevents poor performance." So right from the start, he thought out the best ways to achieve that goal. He put together a small group of imaginative, quick-thinking senior students under the leadership of a house prefect, who every student considered to be the doyen of all manner of riddle-solving. The greatest task before all the participants, he adjudged, was finding out the correct locations to search for the hidden clues, and so he admonished this group to decipher, as much as possible, through brainstorming and riddle-solving techniques the most probable locations for hidden clues.

Next he assembled a group of indomitable sprinters and gave them the task of running like mad to appropriate locations to search for hidden clues. The third or last small group he constituted was made up of scouts. The scouts were students capable of sniffing up the actual trails followed by the other competing teams, especially if they were successful at finding clue locations.

"We must all ensure that Warri House comes first." Burke never failed to encourage his groups at every moment. "Remember the Alamo!" he would say sometimes.

Some students asked what he meant by those words.

"Never mind," he answered, "Let's just say it's a war cry when you're fighting to win a war, after losing a battle." His refrain soon caught on with many participants of the groups, and at times the participants as a whole would shout it out and create a stir among the other competitors in the treasure hunt.

Burke and the leaders of the small groups he formed during the treasure hunt always came together to plan their next approach, like a war office. None of the other houses came near to Warri House in overall organisation for this exciting event.

CHAPTER 20

Majority of the class one boys like Christopher Nomo felt lost in the game. Too junior to be among the core group of senior boys that brainstormed over possible clue locations, and unable to keep pace with the big boys who raced out in search of clues (many of whom were the great athletes of the time), Christopher, thus, found himself in the fringe of the overall game. Soon he was disenchanted and, of all the class one boys, he alone drifted into a parallel activity of his own.

Like a supernumerary, Christopher occupied himself with thinking his way through what could have really happened to their unfortunate schoolmate, Bede Olo. How intriguing it must be that a young boy could age mysteriously, so fast. Until now, he hadn't heard of such an occurrence. The only incident vaguely akin to this that he knew about was that of a maternal uncle, who had not reached forty at the time, but whose hair had all turned grey in a space of a month. It was later on that he learned how that uncle had undergone life-threatening stress related to his work and family, but premature aging for a four-teen-year-old boy was entirely something new.

And for the unfortunate young boy, what was the probability that his sudden aging could be reversed? Christopher reflected, as the questions and riddles kept tumbling through his mind.

To be sure, a drastic change or transformation occurred to an erstwhile fourteen-year-old boy. What agency could be responsible for such an act? No doubt, it wasn't an act of God. What if it was the workings of a mean-spirited human being equipped with some devilish power and possessed of an evil motive? How did this evil transformation come about? This day, in which the unusual event occurred, was unique. Every student was at the soccer field about the time of the strange incidence, every student except the victim of this change himself, Bede Olo.

Something tugged at his mind. How did the person (whoever did this to Bede) leave the busy school campus without a trace? The person may have been using some diabolical means, which may have affected the victim, perhaps in such a way that the victim being quite asleep at the time couldn't at all stir awake or resist the intruder. But who else could have seen the person? The rest of the students were in the soccer field.

That something tugged at his mind again. At the same time, a shadowy figure floated through his mind's eye. He struggled to bring it into focus, and then he remembered: the binoculars, no, the bush path leading to the forest! It had to be that stealthy old man that he nearly bumped into as he raced towards the soccer field to give the principal's binoculars to the head of school.

With the benefit of hindsight and awakened instinct, Christopher knew instantly that the stealthy old man was responsible for the ugly transformation that had occurred to Bede Olo. But how could it be reversed, even if they could not get hold of that sinister man? His heart began to thump violently within his chest at the mere thought, and then a strange calmness overwhelmed him, as so often happened after a spasm.

Christopher thought again, more calmly now. Perhaps, overturning that sudden disease of aging for Bede Olo was now not only a matter of course, but also a matter of extreme urgency, requiring, maybe, several forays in the right direction, including retracing the likely route followed by that stealthy old man as he made his getaway.

Little did Christopher know just how close he had come to the truth.

CHAPTER 21

Bede Olo, sitting just outside the spare room in the principal's boy's quarters, not far from the three policemen presently watching him, thought he heard a loud din of renewed sporting activity among the students. But how unusual; it was as if the whole student population was occupied with some nocturnal recreational activity, not unlike a soccer match; save there were no loud cheers alternated with lulls of muteness or acquiescent watchfulness. That was when the students had just broken up in groups in the school cadets' parade ground and were racing all over the school campus in characteristic, war-like fashion, to search for clue number one. Most students went about with shouts of exuberance and some others simply screamed some familiar muster words, "He ha!"

What could the students be up to this time? Bede wondered. He couldn't help reflecting on his present secluded state. The last time he stayed out of a common school activity, he reminded himself, he ended up becoming an outcast—one now constantly watched by six policemen, or a shift of three of them during meal times. In the event of another school activity, he had foresworn to himself not to stay away, whatever it would take. Despite the fact that he was now watched by the police, he would somehow have to outwit these unwelcomed sentinels and find himself in the thick of the current, on-going school recreational activity—period. His mind set to work immediately. From inside the spare room, he carefully drew a mat near the open doorway and laid down on it, as if to catch some of the cool evening breeze to facilitate sleep. He took care not to upset the plate and cup he had just used for his meal.

Meanwhile, his large bat-like ears with radar sensitivity tuned in on the goings on around him, especially as it concerned the three policemen sitting nearby. None of them suspected he could be up to any tricks, having found him to be docile most of this time. Each one now took his favourite reclined position to snooze. It did not take long before they were all soundly asleep, as if by a mysterious intervention of providence, all to aid Bede Olo's next, determined move.

Bede now raised his head slowly and studied with care the immediate boys' quarters surroundings. There was no one else around, and the three policemen appeared to be quite asleep. He soon came out of the room and moved under the shadows, heading initially in the direction of the main bungalow of the principal's staff quarters before making a detour around the particular boys' quarters building, and then he headed in the direction of the school classroom blocks. Except for his rather slow gait, his stealth was perfectly executed. He just could not move fast.

As Bede left the grounds of the boy's quarters, the other three policemen arrived back from the dining hall where they had their dinner. Seeing all was quiet and their three colleagues, who were watching Bede, soundly asleep, the three policemen were tempted to think everything was alright. As two of them began to prepare positions to recline against and sleep, the sergeant, their leader, who so far detested their role in the matter of the changed boy, decided to inspect the spare room with its door yawning open. This small detail was not uncharacteristic in itself, except there was also that uncanny stillness in the room, of which the open door was only a harbinger—like there was no one inside. He now entered the room in haste and immediately shone his torch to see around it. The bare mat and the dirty plates lying on the floor seemed to mock at him. He raised an alarm.

"Where Caesar? Where the old man? Corporal, wake everyone. The man done escape!"

The sergeant and his men now stirred themselves from their previous lackadaisical attitude. At precisely that moment, Bede Olo was taking elaborate short cuts, first through the grounds of the principal's staff quarters and across the Appian Way between two of the senior staff quarters along that main access to and from the school campus. It did not take him long to find himself in the central area of the campus where the school classroom blocks stood. Later, he would find a place to lurk until he identified a student to assist him in his quest to be fully reintegrated into the student population.

Stanley Osa was the first to reach the clue at the old concrete water tank. He recalled some tit-bits of the conversation between Chisel Face and the head of school back in the latter's corner in the long "A" dormitory. That recall, aided by his imagination, made him move in the direction of the old water tank. When he got to it, he hesitated, seeing it had no external lighting at all. The old water tank looked all the more like a relic from a bygone era. He soon found the object clue in a not-too-accessible underside of a beam in the tank's support structure. He copied out quickly the statement written on it: "I stand here now an old, empty water tank."

Before Stanley finished reading the clue, a huge throng of students raced towards the water tank. He made his exit from the area ahead of this crowd and raced back towards the cadets' parade ground.

CHAPTER 22

Led by the sergeant with a scar, the six policemen decided all on their own to re-apprehend the run-away Bede Olo, without alerting the school authorities. No point, they reasoned, in creating a stir and earning themselves an unwanted reprimand. Perhaps, after they captured their quarry, they could tell the head of school about the development, and at the same time chip in a bit or so on their gallantry demonstrated by re-apprehending their ward.

They now formed three pairs: one to search through all the dormitories, another to move with the rest of the students now engaged in some form of nocturnal recreational activity, and the third to go about at random throughout the rest of the school campus looking into such places as the classrooms, athletic or sports fields and the like.

One after the other, the three small groups of policemen moved out of the boys' quarters and out of the grounds of the principal's staff quarters, as subtly as possible. The sergeant was at the head of the first group. As soon as all six of them regrouped just a little distance away from the principal's staff quarters, the policemen moved quickly towards the terminal end of the Appian Way. From here they would disperse in pairs, according to the search area pre-assigned to each pair.

Near the cluster of signposts at the end of the Appian Way, the policemen encountered a motley group of students who appeared to be gathering for some clandestine activity. The leader was addressing the group of students.

"We will disturb the campus repose by rattling the principal," he said to a chorus of students shouting, "Yea! Yea!"

"His administration is too much of a throwback to the days of the Royal Niger Company - where matters, however sensitive, were just allowed to peter out. We will not have it so this time, especially now that a student has mysteriously changed to an old man of sixty. Just think, it could have been anyone of us."

The leader's speech seemed to charge up the group of students, as each of them was now moved to take up the gauntlet. Quite suddenly, the students all began to chant, "We want Bede! We want Bede!" Simultaneously, they began to match up the Appian Way and head towards the principal's staff quarters.

Stanley hastened back to the cadets' parade ground to report on clue number one, which he found. He avoided the throng of students that surged like head waters towards the disused water tank. Instead of going the shorter route between the sick bay and the water tank on the one side, and Forcados, Warri and School Houses on the other side, he took a detour around the back of both the water tank and the sick bay.

Already, Stanley heard the strange chants, "We want Bede! We want Bede!" As he came close to the cluster of signs at the terminal end of the Appian Way, he heard the noise louder and saw it came from a group of students who looked like demonstrators marching up the Appian Way. But where were they heading to—the main gate? That didn't make sense. Perhaps the demonstrators were marching aimlessly along the Appian Way for want of a focus, or else to air their grievances among the group of senior teachers, including the arts master who resided along that main thoroughfare. If the demonstrators were really desperate, however, they could be marching all the way to the principal's staff quarters. To be sure, all of this spelt trouble.

Stanley felt he had to alert the head of school immediately. He warned the senior prefect earlier—and Chisel Face coincidentally corroborated the same warning—but the senior prefect did not take the matter seriously, it would appear. Now see what was happening. He couldn't help recalling the classic example of a warning that fell on deaf ears with fatal consequences in Shakespeare's *Julius Caesar*. On his way to the Capitol, Caesar remarked to Soothsayer, "The Ides of March are come." To that, Soothsayer answered, "Ay, Caesar; but not gone.

CHAPTER 23

As Stanley passed by the copse of trees near the arterial roads that joined the Appian Way, he heard a huff of a noise. It could have come from a man, and Stanley soon discovered the human voice, at certain decibels, nuance or degree of modulation was the easiest give away of one who didn't quite belong. Above the cacophony of sounds emanating from the treasure hunt, the nascent student demonstration and the campus in late evening repose, Stanley searched for the source of this strange sound.

It came from near the power station. Impatiently, he looked and saw a shadowy figure of a man standing under a tree—away from the glare of the outside light, but closer to the mechanical drawing building.

"I need some help. Don't be afraid. I am Bede Olo," said the stranger to Stanley, somewhat hesitantly.

Stanley did not reply a word.

"My problem is that everyone thinks I have changed to someone else," said the stranger again, more hesitantly.

Stanley still kept silent, though inwardly, he was beginning to feel more impatient.

"I just evaded the six policemen detailed to watch me in a spare room in the principal's boys' quarters. Now I want to find out what really happened to me."

"I don't believe you," Stanley said to the stranger.

"But I'm telling you the truth."

"May be you are. But I can't help you. You must go and see the head of school."

"Where can I find him?"

"He's at the cadets' parade ground."

"But I'm Bede. I don't know how else to convince you or anyone else for that matter."

"See the head of school. He can handle this matter better."

"He can't solve my problem, except perhaps to request from the principal that I be left alone—left unhounded until I've found out what really happened to me."

"As you wish," Stanley said. He would have bolted off, but a question from the stranger delayed him.

"What was that cry, 'We want Bede!' about?"

"Sorry, you can find out for yourself."

The riot scene they just witnessed made the six policemen feel they were definitely now in a quandary. The sergeant with the scar asked his men to forget about chasing after the run-away Bede, and think about how to quell the unexpected demonstration. He also detailed a corporal among his men to move quickly and inform the principal's butler about the student demonstrators heading towards the principal's staff quarters. He and his men would do their utmost to quell this revolt, before it could degenerate into a complete breakdown of law and order around the school campus. With that done, the sergeant and the rest of his men now went straight to counter the group of rioters.

With an unsteady but loud voice, the sergeant accosted the student demonstrators. "This . . . this is . . . a . . . a warning. Disperse . . . disperse, I say . . . and you will not be harmed. Disperse . . . at once!" As he shouted out his warning in broken bits, the sergeant readied a canister of tear gas, or smoke bomb.

The group of student demonstrators, initially taken aback, now mouthed their earlier chants with renewed gusto: "We want Bede! We want Bede!" The students also continued their match forward, unimpeded.

The sergeant shouted his warnings again and again, until his voice became hoarse. Then the students swarmed around the group of five policemen.

The sergeant released the tear gas canister, which sounded in a huge tod, before it began to puff out white smoke. The student demonstrators abandoned marching and chanting, and scampered to safety leaving the policemen to inhale the tear gas, as they themselves had no protective face masks. But the students soon regrouped.

CHAPTER 24

To Stanley's surprise, the cadets' parade ground was a beehive of students when he arrived back there. Some other students had beaten him to first place in reporting the discovery of clue number one. He felt anguish and wished he could exact some penalty for this development caused by the delay of him being accosted by that stranger who claimed he was Bede Olo.

Still feeling angry and disappointed, Stanley went to the head of school to tell him about the man impersonating Bede, whom he met near the mechanical drawing building. He also told the head of school about the group of student demonstrators.

Following his report to the head of school, Stanley saw the senior prefect hand over the proceedings, including score sheets for the treasure hunt game, to Chisel Face, before immediately hurrying off towards the scene of the student demonstration.

Stanley inquired after the search words for clue number two and subsequently noted them down in his pocket notebook: "The darkest hour is just before the dawn."

He began to recite those search words, while at the same time his mind raced ahead of him to possible places around the school campus evocative of deep darkness, or whatever else it was, that pointed to the darkness and evil surrounding the changed Bede Olo. The latter part of his hunch although topical did not seem feasible, and could not have been what either Chisel Face or the head of school had in mind—whichever of them wrote this particular clue. Thus resolved, Stanley went on his way in search of clue number two, groping still for whatever pointed to deep darkness. But within him there was this testy feeling, it's now going to be "fire on the mountain," for the good ol'head of school, and for my humble self. No wonder it is said that "a stitch in time saves nine."

Bede Olo became increasingly restless. How long was he going to lurk in the shadows? Being a fugitive as it were? It would have been better had he done something really wrong to warrant his fate. But not so; instead, he was a fugitive of some sort—his proper, well-known personality having metamorphosed into a weird old man as other students seemed to be telling him. He had not really noticed any change in his face when he had looked in his mirror back at the dormitory, however, but then that could also have been part of whatever happened to him. The mirror, too, could have been jinxed.

Within him, he felt as though time was running out, and he just had to, somehow, resolve this dilemma and get to the bottom of whatever happened to him that cost him the sense of belonging. Even a moment earlier when he appealed to that impatient senior student, there was that sense of foreboding. It dawned on him that the senior student would not have any qualms whatsoever in betraying him. So much then for his attempt to identify a concerned student to assist him find out what ever happened to him.

On an instinct, Bede moved away from near the mechanical drawing building. Where, only a moment ago, he stood to talk with that facetious senior student. And now he was upstairs in a room overlooking the cadets' parade ground or drill quad. From there, he hoped that he could pick out sufficient "feelers" from that vantage position to warn him on his next move, without being found out. Still, he knew he needed assistance from a student he could trust, an ally of some sort, but so far none.

As it turned out, the matching piece for herald clue number two was to be Stanley's quickest discovery for the entire treasure hunt game—and it happened in quite inauspicious circumstances.

Whilst contemplating the areas around the school campus most evocative of deep darkness, he was not aware of his drifting close to the assembly hall. By contrast, the assembly hall area was the most bright, well-lit area on campus at night.

It was by the assembly hall, as he saw the night watchman go to the belfry to ring the ninth hour, that Stanley stirred back to present reality. Seeing at once how far from his predetermined course he drifted, Stanley decided to look around the belfry just on the spur of the moment.

The decision paid off, and there, by one of the four columns holding up the belfry he discovered the matching piece to clue number two. On it was written quite a mouthful: "Diffraction and the 'halo' effect lead to lightening of the night sky in every locality, until just before dawn."

As Stanley left the precinct of the belfry, the night watchman told him of another group that had been the first, ahead of him, in discovering that clue by the belfry. Stanley thanked the night watchman for the information and hastened toward the cadets' quad to report on his latest find. No more interceptions, he prayed, but wondered within him, whether or not that stranger who intercepted him on his way to reporting clue number one was not a sort of decoy—one meant to get him off target. *No point crying over spilt milk*, he told himself. However, he had to be more vigilant from now on.

Rorvi Yough, a soft spoken senior boy from Orerokpe House, remembered seeing from afar a lonely figure by the uncompleted swimming pool earlier in the evening. After the treasure hunt got well under way, he thought to review all the search words for clues and see which one was remotely connected to the swimming pool. He found he had a little difficulty deciding which one. However, after the clue number one was discovered by the disused overhead water tank, he concluded that the only other receptacle must be the unfinished swimming pool. He went over there and was rewarded to see the piece of paper with the answer for clue number six.

On it was written the words, "Eureka! Eureka!" ("I have found it! I have found it!"), cried the scientist Archimedes, as he ran naked with excitement out of his bath, all the way home. The occasion occurred after the king or ruler requested him to find a method for determining whether a crown was pure gold or alloyed with silver. Archimedes realized, as he stepped into his bath, that a given weight of gold would displace less water than an equal weight of silver (which is less dense than gold).

CHAPTER 25

For the first time in nearly ten months, since the principal handpicked him to be the head of school, Gerald Egbe now had his first serious misgivings. He wondered to himself now if it had been a good idea in the first place to have accepted the position without asking any questions whatsoever. He couldn't really have rejected it. Just as the idea of having prefects was a *sine qua non* in a body of students, so, too, rejecting the position of a senior school prefect, for that matter, was totally out of the question. Many of the schoolteachers would have said to him, "You must be out of your mind."

So, he accepted the appointment and he never looked back; not until now. Also, most of the time it was a thankless job. And if it was not tough enough, the situation that he then faced at the scene of the student demonstration could make the school authorities, literally, ask for his head to be taken off his shoulders—and that from a hasty decision, especially if he failed to bring this mess of a student demonstration under control and revert the entire student body to normalcy, as though he was to blame for all this confusion. *Don't panic*, he told himself, as he got ready to address the crowd of student demonstrators.

"I implore you, please calm down and let us discuss your grievances."

The students shouted him down.

"None of your glib talking," one student called out with effrontery.

"We don't want live and let die," another chipped in, still on a note of confrontation, however banal.

At that instant, the head of school looked down, allowing his gaze to wonder over his sturdy feet. It was a gesture of humility at such times that somehow also showed abject self-repudiation. And then, he summoned from deep within his being that extraordinary courage that marked him out. He told himself, *Somehow, I must douse the tense situation before me and revert this group of errant students to their usual law-abiding selves.* Then it occurred to him to change his manner of handling the rabble-rousers.

"If you are on the side of redress, move out of the crowd to my right-hand side. I have a proposition that will interest you, and that could, this very night, lead to resolving the mystery around Bede Olo, our unfortunate colleague."

No one moved.

Some of the students who heard him speak, now debated amongst themselves the merit of his latest pronouncements, and the real motive behind his words. Some said it was a ploy to isolate and deal with the ringleaders in the crowd. Others said it was only fair to hear him out; after all, many got on this demonstration to try and get redress. A break-up into moderates and hardliners now threatened the entire crowd of student demonstrators, and the head of school took advantage of the situation to press forward his case.

"Seriously, I am committed to what I am saying. If you know you would rather take part, this night, in resolving the mysterious change that happened to our student colleague, please move to my right-hand side."

The crowd of student demonstrators quietened down considerably, long enough for the head of school to add the uncompromising rider, "Or, perhaps some of you are not really seeking redress. Should that be the case, then continue in your current course of action. Go on then with this unreasonable demonstration and see where it gets you. I assure you, those who prove to be too heady will be rusticated."

At this juncture, there was absolute quiet such that any accidental drop of a pin on the coal tar would have been heard. None of the students moved. And then, as sudden as it ceased, the noise resumed with the pitter-patter of many students all talking at once. Some students began to separate themselves to the right-hand side of the head of school. These students now parting ways with the old cause were frowned at by the rest of the demonstrators, as though they were committing high treason. The initial separation further triggered the process of added separation. Thus, the recalcitrant ones among the demonstrators could do absolutely nothing to stop this breakup of the entire crowd of demonstrators. The moderates won, and all the rest could do was to fume in exasperation while the break up exercise lasted. At last, this process was completed, and among all the students who separated from the group of demonstrators, the head of school chose five senior boys. He requested the five senior boys to accompany him. The large number of students who separated from the entire crowd of demonstrators effectively ended the incident.

CHAPTER 26

Before the student demonstration finally expired, the unrepentant leader tried to show his frustration at the way the affair died down rather abruptly, after the head of school's intervention, by picking a personal quarrel with the form-five student who was one of the first to break away from his group.

"You turncoat," he said aggressively as he grabbed at this other form-five student.

"Take your stinking hands off me, or I'll report you." This other form-five student fought back tenaciously, trying to pull away from the erstwhile leader of the demonstrators. His shirt, however, appeared seized with a vice-like grip by his aggressor. Now in a panic, he began to pull himself every which way, just to break out from that terrible grip.

"Break it up now." The head of school took his time before calling a halt to the scuffle. The leader of the demonstrators let go without much ado. By then much of the crowd had dispersed.

"Listen all of you!" the head of school said raising his voice. "Just go over to the cadets' parade ground now. You have to participate in the treasure hunt."

The head of school then spoke to the five students he chose, asking them to follow him. "Officers," the senior school prefect called out to the policemen at the same time, "I need two of your men to accompany us also."

Two of the policemen stepped forward. Soon afterwards, the senior prefect began to herd his small band, comprising the five senior students and the two policemen, in the direction of the forest.

When they got to the school's perimeter fence and before they entered the forest, the senior prefect paused momentarily.

Ahead of them was this amalgam of darkness. It stretched on unbroken. Even the several torch lights they aimed in that direction only heightened the feeling of uncertainty. None of them could easily tell the trees from the forest, the climbers and ferns from the shrubs and tall grasses.

The senior school prefect paused a little longer to train his ears. He saw the ubiquitous presence of glow worms; he heard the strident and insistent crackle of crickets and the punctuating cry of what some local people call "bush babies" and other low-life denizens. These all together appeared to voice out a presentiment to unwary humans like him and the others he was leading. The forced rhythm, with which these creatures sounded or appeared, only heightened that presentiment.

His uncle, a renowned hunter of small game, once told him that such sounds served as a sort of compass for a hunter at night, and simply so because they were more pronounced when one had not yet fully entered the forest. Once inside the forest, however, the same sounds seemed more diffused. And that, in any case, if the sounds seized altogether momentarily, then one had better watch out—for it was most certain that either a predatory beast was within striking distance, or else a spirit being was on the prowl.

As the head of school and his small band of people entered the forest, he found it very unnerving just because of what his uncle told him. He could do nothing about it, he surmised, but also found it impossible to dislodge the thought of it from his mind. As for their foray into the forest this time of night, he did not really plan the mission. He simply would have to count on the unexpected.

Just as the events leading to it were all unexpected. Still he would not want his band of people to keep a vigil in the forest this night, while the treasure hunt, which was a better event that he had planned, was proceeding without him under the supervision of the head of Oleh House. Therefore, whatever had to happen in the forest this night better happen quickly, so that they, the students in his small band, could get back to the campus and join the treasure hunt. The policemen would then of course go back to their beat. Haven resolved that in his mind, he asked the students and the two policemen to try and find out clues of the old man reportedly seen entering the forest earlier that evening.

"Remember," he told them, "the thin old man was seen wearing a faded danshiki and a homespun loin cloth. Anything you find should help us to solve the riddle of the changed boy."

With that said by the senior school prefect, everyone now got busy for a while.

CHAPTER 27

"Two down, eight more to go," Burke said to members of his house by way of announcing the discovery of clue number two, located at the belfry by one of their own participants. One thing about the treasure hunt that was fast becoming real was there was no time for post-mortems. Like in a gruelling exam session, as long as there remained even a single paper to be written (or in this case so many clues lying out there undiscovered), the beat just had to go on. And the teams had to keep going after the undiscovered clues, until the end.

Regardless of this pressure, Burke felt disposed to enjoy all of the thrill and the ultimate conquest in finding out each clue. That bit about the Alamo was none the worse, after all, for a well-placed metaphor to ginger up his team members.

"Remember the Alamo!" he said to them for the umpteenth time, and then as soon as he said that every member of his team took his cue. The search parties, considered the vanguard of the entire dormitory's participation, waited eagerly for the think tank members including Burke himself, for fresh locations to search for clue number three. Some of the scouts in his team moved around and cocked their ears; perchance, they might pick up something very useful.

"Hello there," Burke called to one of the scouts, his brain engaged in the critical activity of identifying, sorting and whittling out poor clue locations. "Be vigilant, and don't fail to report to me if another house becomes the front runner other than our own house."

Up till the discovery of clue number two, Warri House remained the leader, followed by School House, although the participation in School House boiled down to the efforts of only one person—Stanley Osa. Still, Stanley, considered the lone ranger for School House, was a threat to Warri House with its ambition of winning first overall position in the game.

Oleh and Ashaka Houses were behind those two front runners in the potential for finding out clues quickly. Sapele House was next to Oleh and Ashaka Houses, followed by Orerokpe House. Forcados House, unfortunately, was bringing up the rear right from the start.

The third clue sent most participants in all the houses, except Stanley, on a wild goose chase. It read, "Who is that O-leap-ian?"

Urged by some of the participants, the head of Oleh House also read out the search words for clue number four, namely, "*L'Etat C'est Moi.*"

"L' . . . what?" some students questioned.

The senior Oleh House prefect beamed to himself. "Wait till I'll be telling you *E pluribus Unum,*" he said and then explained the meaning of the words for the clue number four: "'The state or nation is I'—a famous quotation of a flamboyant French King."

The students began immediately to huddle together in their groups, brainstorming and identifying possible search locations, while the energetic racers waited impatiently to dash off in the soon-to-be-identified locations to search for clue number three.

Stanley soon got on his way, thinking deeply as he went. If anything, he learnt a cardinal lesson in the way and manner he located the matching piece for clue number two. *Things are not always what they seem to be*, he said to himself repeatedly, as he contemplated where to search for clue number three. For once, he paid grudging tribute to the combined genius of the head of school and Chisel Face. *Where in the world had these two odd fellows dredged up these tough puzzles for the treasure hunt?* he wondered. And for these two school prefects to have had all the clues creatively strung-up together—like some rich tapestry, poking quizzically at the learning and societal mores in various age—was pure genius.

But where now should he search to find the matching piece for clue number three? That was the one million naira question.

He did not exactly stumble upon the answer. Rather, he reasoned in his mind to unravel the mystery. The pavilion and athletics field both beckoned as he thought to himself, *Surely these are the obvious places to search.* But then, his mind told him differently. So he did not go to the pavilion, nor did he go to the athletics field. Those areas were some of the farthest locations on campus, and were very isolated from the hub of the inhabited campus, where most of the treasure hunt was taking place.

Now, "leap" had a revealing ring to it, like leaping over a fence or across an obstacle, especially in haste—to avoid possible apprehension. Stanley thought deeply, and at the same time the vice principal's usual refrain while announcing the names of students, who were caught breaking bounds, rang in his mind's ear, "As I always say, your sins shall find you out." All of this triggered his mind, and in a flash of intuition, Stanley now had the answer.

He hastened toward the big ditch that carried storm water to the streams in the eastern fringe of the campus. And sure enough, there on a warning stake he found the object clue number three. He also discovered the matching piece for clue number four pasted on a window of the principal's office. He was elated by this seeming harvest of two clues within so short a time and bounded toward the cadets' quad like he was walking on air.

In the meantime, two senior boys from Warri House arrived at the pavilion to search for clue number three as well. One of the two shielded his candle, which he held out to the other, as both of them anxiously searched every column and wall on the top main stand of the pavilion. The two boys stood near the middle of the pavilion, and as both began to lose hope, one of them heard some faint noise in the distance and he turned to see.

"Do you see other boys coming here to search for clue number three?" asked the other sprinter, who kept himself busy searching without turning around to see the source of noise both of them heard.

"I see one . . . two . . . three or more torch lights. Some people are coming down the road. But they don't appear to be in a hurry."

The busy student now turned around reluctantly.

"Those are not treasure hunters. But then, where does that leave us?"

"Our scouts should have something for us by now," said the first student who saw the torches and people coming towards them. "Let's go back to them."

The other boy agreed, and both boys soon took off toward the cadets' parade ground.

The longer the head of school stayed out of supervising the treasure hunt game, the more the head of Oleh House warmed up to his own inevitable role as "anchor man" for the entire recreation. At the onset when the senior prefect handed the proceedings and score sheets to him, the head of Oleh House did have his own misgivings. By the time most participants turned in answers for clue number three, however, the Oleh house senior prefect began to relax and even to indulge the odd feeling that he may not have to hand back the supervision of the game to the head of school—the game's *de jure* captain. That feeling or thought triggered yet another, and another, in an ever expansive and widening circle of rapture, which now enveloped his mind.

Much of the activity relating to the recreation evolved directly or indirectly from his effort. Although it was the head of school alone who came up with the idea of a treasure hunt, but he wrote most of the clues, and many of the brilliant ones. Perhaps, it was only natural that destiny should thrust upon him also the supervision of the actual game. Oddly, the Oleh House senior prefect fancied himself as a modern-day, schoolboy version of Alexis de Tocqueville, a French statesman and chronicler of democracy in America. Although nothing he penned for the treasure hunt could compare with the famous French statesman's classic, *Democracy in America*, there was that persistent and indulgent thought in his mind.

"Imagine that 'Gone are the days…' could very well be indicative of 'the tyranny of public opinion.' Or, my scrupulous observation of the proceedings thus far in the game would reverberate with the inescapable idea that 'majority rule could be as oppressive as the rule of a despot'– never mind The Bill of Rights where it exists, not to mention, if it didn't exist."

His reverie came to an abrupt end as Stanley appeared to report the pair of clues he just discovered.

CHAPTER 28

"I've found three and four," Stanley muttered.
"Go on. What do they say?"

"Three says, 'True heroes are anonymous,' and four says, 'Many sun kings.'"

"Okay. Listen now for search words for clue numbers five, six and seven. Ready?"

"Yea," Stanley hummed.

One student who stood nearby and heard Stanley announce the results for clues three and four left immediately to inform the racers in Warri House, but he couldn't find any of them around. "Clue number five reads, 'The words that I speak unto you, they are spirit and they are life, so says the Master. Spirit and life are represented by this popular school effigy. What is this effigy?' Clue number six reads, 'This great man of science, is reputed to have, on one occasion, run out of his bathtub adorned only in his birthday suit. What was the occasion? Find out from the unfinished receptacle of a material versatile for bathing, sporting and travel.' Clue number seven: 'The ratio of the sines of these two related angles in optics is a constant for a material medium, as defined by a scientific law. Two approaches to a central edifice on the campus subtend angles, with imaginary lines of sight, that give the value of this constant for air. Locate the two approaches.'"

"How about reading out the rest of the clues, numbers eight, nine and ten?" Stanley asked.

"Yes. You can have everything at once if you want. Clue number eight says, 'This form of government has no dogma. An adherent is considered a pragmatist, but is by nature a sceptic. I am a portal of a room where a replica of this form of government takes place. What am I?' Clue number nine: 'Here, love, deuce and advantage are commonplace expressions for tally.'

And clue number ten says, 'Always be nasty to young people.' This is the moral obverse of an otherwise sound advice by a famous Irish playwright to a group of graduating sixth-form students. Where is this advice posted?"

Stanley took a deep breath as Chisel Face finished reading out the search words for all the remaining clues. He jotted down only the keywords and as he left the grounds of the cadets' quad, his mind was racing. Slowly now he mulled over the key search words, starting with those of clue number seven.

Regardless of the treasure hunt, the words "a central edifice." conjured up in his mind just one image. That of the imposing assembly hall with its herringbone patterned parquet floor and nothing else, so he went over there to have a close look at the two covered approach walkways. On one of the columns lining the approach from the direction of the main school block, he found written on a small piece of paper, the words "refractive index." *Quite cryptic*, he thought inwardly, while somewhat urged on by those two words, he went ahead to inspect the approach from the direction of the science block and there on one of the posts supporting the covered walkway he found another small piece of paper with the words "Snell's Law."

Seemingly triumphant now, Stanley decided to press on for clue numbers five and six. He would, with some luck, search out these two additionally before reporting his cumulative finds. And if everything went as planned, he would then be left with clue numbers eight through ten. These last three he would attack with the ferocity of a caged cat, and again with any luck, he would get rid of them quickly—like they were a real nuisance by then. Once out of the way, he would delight himself with the sweet savour of victory, while he waited the concluding dance party and the award of gifts and prizes.

Thus resolved, Stanley proceeded to search for clue number five. He, however, had to change his plan.

Out of boredom, Christopher Nomo drifted away from the activities of the treasure hunt. He sought temporary respite upstairs in the main school block overlooking the cadets' parade ground.

A long while ago, he informed the head of school about the strange old man whom he had seen scurrying off the campus and entering the forest near the broken down portion of the school's perimeter fence. That was when he returned from fetching the principal's binoculars during the day's soccer match.

Abstracted, Christopher considered two immediate choices for his own movement as he surveyed the cadets' parade ground, which now was in temporary repose. Visiting his cousin, Stanley Osa, as he was invited to do was out of the question due to the treasure hunt. He couldn't quit the treasure hunt altogether at this juncture, even if he wanted to. So what else could he do for real excitement?

Oh, he would have loved to go after that strange old man whom he knew must have induced premature aging in Bede Olo, their fellow schoolboy. That proposition was, however, impracticable for personal safety reasons and the requirement to obey school rules at all times; yet, the thought just wouldn't go away.

What would be the risks involved in embarking on a solo mission into the forest in search of the old man? He could meet with some misfortune, some harm from wild beasts or even from such a diabolical old man. But risks aside, he could obtain some valuable information to resolve the mystery of the changed schoolboy.

He hit the tip of his right foot, as he tried to step up the stairs leading to the upper level of the main school block. And that, for the moment, put a prompt quietus on all his ruminations.

But where was the head of school? Since he informed him about that furtive old man, he had not seen much of the senior prefect around the cadets' parade ground. The last he heard, he in fact had put down that sudden demonstration by some students and since gone after some other business. Where else could he have gone? Could he, perhaps, be trying to track down the sinister old man? Well, he, would go upstairs in the main school block and wait, until he could find out the exact disposition of the senior school prefect.

CHAPTER 29

As Christopher emerged on the landing upstairs, he was sharply reminded of a notorious jester who belonged to one of the classrooms nearby. This stubby boy's antics ranged from the zany to the surreal, evanescent ways of getting school boys to laugh. Who else, but only this small stubby boy, could successfully bait the bigger boys in the class and remain unscathed. The small stubby boy did all that with his daily dose of lampoon, cartoon quips, and caricatures. He never stopped poking fun at the big boys with the sole intent of cleverly exposing foibles in each one's character and personality or else highlighting obvious physical imbalances.

Maybe he could somehow also thwart that sinister old man without being hurt, but how? Then Christopher suddenly halted, in his tracks.

Someone just moved from the corridor into a nearby classroom in the dark.

Except for the outside lighting near the bursar's office, the school block had most of its light switched off. However, someone was lurking on the corridor. And whoever it was just moved into the nearby classroom as he moved along the corridor.

Christopher now sailed on tip toes towards the particular classroom, where the shadowy figure was and moved to switch on the lights.

"Please don't" came the words from a strained voice. "I'm only hiding here until I can decide what to do with myself."

"Who are you?"

"B-e-d-e . . ." answered the tired voice with hesitation.

"Bede, I know what must have happened to you. At least, I think it is that sinister old man I saw making a break for the forest this afternoon that must have caused all that you are now suffering."

"Do you know where I can find him?"

"No. But wait. I have an idea." Christopher left Bede and rushed down to the cadets' quad on the ground below. He returned a few minutes later to talk with Bede.

"I think you and I should try and retrace the footpath or route that the sinister old man must have taken to make his getaway, right from that moment by your bed after he carried out his diabolical operation on you."

"Let's go then," Bede said. His voice was upbeat, though tired still.

Christopher put his scouting faculties in top gear and before long they moved to the Common Room in Sapele House. From there they found their way to the school's perimeter fence, while taking care to avoid the hordes of students moving here and there in search of clues.

Two senior boys from Sapele House who were subtly searching for clues around the tennis courts in front of the dining hall caught Stanley's eye. He abandoned the plan he had earlier decided on for realizing all his clues. Very swiftly, he moved over to the tennis courts on the heels of those two senior boys from Sapele House. This decision, apparently rash though, paid off very quickly. And out of it, Stanley now added the answer to clue number nine to his small cache of clues he discovered.

The immediate problem he now faced was how to report on the three clues he found, and set off again to search for the remaining four. A queue built up in front of Chisel Face, and precious time was now spent in reporting clues. Stanley, however, finished reporting the clues he found, and he went off again in search of the remaining ones.

As Christopher Nomo and Bede Olo finally moved closer to the forest on the heels of the head of school and his group, after retracing that sinister old man's getaway route, there were some telling changes wrought on Bede. Christopher Nomo first noticed it in his sprightly walk, and in a husky turn of his voice every now and then. Still he couldn't tell much if anything else was really happening. He supposed that in a jinxed situation such as he felt Bede had been exposed to, the spell or charm or whatever could suddenly be broken and in that case the results could be astounding and could be realised very quickly.

And who knows? Maybe in the short while that both of them were retracing the footsteps of that sinister old man, some extraordinary changes were already happening in this manner. Only time would tell what the final outcome could be in this matter, Christopher concluded as he kept walking alongside Bede.

Both friends walked in silence for a while.

Bede stifled the feeling burning in his mind: He would sooner than later get back to old self.

CHAPTER 30

Burke gave a piece of paper to the Head of Oleh House, asking him to read it. "It's the answer to clue number ten," he added, gasping.

The rest of the members of Warri House waited anxiously. Stanley Osa and many participants from School House were also present.

The senior house prefect of Oleh House read the clue silently:

> *Some of your school fellows may surprise you by getting hanged. Others, of whom you may have the lowest opinion, will turn out to be geniuses, and become the great men of your time. Therefore, always be nice to young people. Some little beast who is no good at games and whose head you may possibly have clouted for indulging a sarcastic wit and a sharp tongue at your expense may grow into a tremendous swell, like Rudyard Kipling. You never can tell.*
>
> —George Bernard Shaw's advice to sixth form students

"Listen, everyone," said the senior prefect of Oleh House after he read that piece of paper, "I need just two more houses to complete the ten clues, and after that I would have to end the treasure hunt officially and proceed with announcing the results followed by the award of prizes."

The senior Ashaka house prefect got some form-four students to set the snacks and prizes on tables brought to the cadets' quad for this purpose. He also arranged for a big stereo cassette radio, operated on a car battery, to be brought to the arena. This would serve as music box for a short dance party to conclude the game.

Shortly afterwards Oleh and Ashaka Houses each came up with its outstanding set of clues to complete the total of ten clues designated for the entire treasure hunt. The head of Oleh House subsequently announced the official end for the game. The fore-runners in the game began to taunt participants from the houses that failed to complete the ten clues.

"Waste pipes" was the familiar lexicon for the underachiev-ers freely bandied by the members in the successful houses.

"Question: would prizes also be given to the waste pipes among us?" one ebullient senior student asked.

"Who are you calling waste pipe?" his friend retorted. "Just because your house is among the winners in the treasure hunt, now you can talk. But don't forget when we beat all of you in cricket."

"Who cares about cricket?"

The banter went on and on for some time. And then the mood shifted to one of merriment as the positions were announced, snacks shared and the prizes were given out.

CHAPTER 31

Standing ground inside the forest was at a premium this night, as the head of school was soon to find out. He ventured outside of a partially waterlogged bush path in the forest to pick a burnt piece of wood, which was curiously lying around without any evidence of having been used in a fireplace. He had to quickly retrace his steps to avoid falling into a murky pool of water. He still got the piece of burnt wood, and as he did so he saw something else, like a piece of cloth, partially submerged. He almost waved it off. However, he at last reached for that piece of cloth, only to find out that it was part of an abandoned pouch. It was made of either goatskin or cowhide.

No sooner had he picked these two items than a grave silence descended on everything around. Nothing stirred in the forest for a brief agonizing moment. Not even the distant echo from the school campus could be heard.

On an impulse, the head of school turned around slowly. Though it was dark, the senior prefect's face suddenly lost its usual composure. His eyes protruded from their sockets like balls of flesh about to fall out of his head. Meanwhile, his strong lower jaw dropped as if the muscles could no longer hold it in position. In that brief agonizing moment, he glimpsed a squat half-creature, half-apparition, but certainly not a human, although one that walked (*or floated?*) erect. The creature's eyes were bloodshot and they seemed to bore right through his scull to reach inside to the back of his head for his thoughts. Right that moment, there was not much residual thought held in the senior prefect's head, at least nothing that could be summed up simply by the word "fear." The whole episode was electrifying and lasted very fleetingly.

It took the senior school prefect a little while to regain his composure, then he looked around to the others in his group, from one of the two policemen who seemed to be holding tenaciously to a twig in the dark, to one senior boy who clasped another's arm awkwardly. He saw men and boys only beginning to stir out of sudden shock.

Whatever just appeared to them, and induced such shock in the men and boys present with him, was probably out to sound a note of warning. He needed nobody else to tell him. He and his group just had to exit the forest, pronto! And that he proceeded to do immediately.

Only he insisted on everyone else moving ahead of him where he could see each person, and in that order, they all hastened out of the forest and re-entered the school campus.

"Oh, what a night!" the head of school said, pausing for breath.

The night's strange occurrences, however, were far from over. A soft voice called from behind them. They all hurried away from it and pushed farther into the campus. Then the senior prefect turned to see the source of the voice, while the others, who stood farther from him, also turned to look.

Standing just beyond the perimeter fence was an old woman with greying hair. She held a lantern glowing in a strange fluorescent hue. Her face was indistinct, but she spoke in the local dialect:

> *Look no further for*
> *What you ought to be seeking:*
> *The soul of a youthful boy or*
> *Gem of another human life*
> *Is restored to him as you shall find*
> *By the next morning light.*

Everything seemed to be happening quickly from then on. Maybe it was all a nightmare, which daylight would shake out of them. But the import of the old woman's words concerning Bede was not lost on the head of school. It was worth the effort of coming into the forest this night then, if really it turned out that the old woman's message was true concerning Bede. That was the outcome he hoped for as he led the small group into the forest this night; however, in the face of that unexpected confrontation with that unearthly presence, he was not so sure about any good outcome.

The morning was only about eight hours away, so it would be worth checking to see the outcome.

Christopher Nomo, hiding with Bede Olo not far from the perimeter fence, panicked at first as he heard the stampede of the small band of people entering the campus. It was the head of school and his group, but the group kept hurrying away from the forest and back into the school campus. Christopher was puzzled. A little later, the group paused to listen to what appeared to be a woman's voice, and by that time the group settled into a somewhat normal pace of walking and there were no hurried footfalls.

Christopher clearly heard the final pronouncements of the woman. Although it puzzled him who she might have been, he felt nevertheless elated by the realization that Bede would be alright by morning, going by what he heard the woman say at last.

By now, Bede was experiencing one of the strangest reactions it would ever be his privilege to undergo since his transformation happened. He couldn't really explain it. Perhaps, it was a sudden burst of energy within or an overflow of hormones. Whatever the cause, it was like a person coming out of a hypnotic dream. Quite inexplicably, too, Bede felt so elated, he wanted to shout it out loud, "I feel alright!"

Due to the reaction still going on inside him, Bede was oblivious of the happenings around both of them, which Christopher followed closely. Later, as he heard the movement of feet at a distance, he turned to Christopher for an explanation.

"It's the head of school and his group. Let's get out of here. They have gone far," Christopher said as both boys came out of their hiding place.

Christopher told Bede they had to hurry up.

"Why?"

"We have to just go far from this forest, of course. I think the head of school and his group saw something in the forest that made them all to rush back into the campus when they did. There was also an old woman's voice that I overheard talking to them."

"But, you know what? I feel alright."

"Let's just get out of here first, and then we can talk about it."

"Thanks, anyway, for your concern this night."

They kept hurrying and only slowed down when they came close to the dining hall. Christopher then proceeded to explain what he overheard that woman's voice say to the senior school prefect and his band of students and policemen.

"I tell you I am alright, even now."

Christopher noted that Bede's voice changed very much from what it sounded like at the beginning when both boys met in the dark, inside one of the classrooms. Now his voice sounded very much like that of a fourteen-year-old boy, and his movements were very much like those of a young boy. Christopher, however, believed that complete change, from being a sixty-year-old man to a fourteen-year-old boy, awaited the morning, just as that woman's voice indicated. But he didn't tell Bede what he thought.

CHAPTER 32

Bede stretched himself on his bed. It was seven in the morning. The bell rang moments ago for reveille. Being Sunday, most students preoccupied themselves with getting to the dining hall on time for breakfast and then going in groups to the churches in the town.

He stretched himself again before getting out of bed. It was only as he got ready to enter the bathroom that he was reminded of the events of the day before. He saw one of the three prefects who was the first to report the incidence of his sudden mysterious aging to the principal. The prefect was coming along the corridor as Bede got ready to enter the bathroom.

On seeing him, the prefect made a shrill noise and began to stare at him in bewilderment. Bede ignored him and entered the bathroom, but the prefect followed him inside. Standing transfixed by the screen wall, the prefect continued to stare at him.

Bede began to feel self-conscious and despairing of what to do next, he tied his towel around his loins. Then the prefect spoke.

"So it's true. Wonders they say will never end," the prefect said in amazement. "They've really turned you back into your boyish self again. Who would have believed it?"

"Please, you're embarrassing me," Bede said. "If you don't mind, I want to take a shower."

The prefect just stood astonished. "You don't know how lucky you are. The only time I have heard of a boy aging prematurely, the boy ended up dying. You are very lucky."

"So I've heard. Can I take a shower now?"

A small crowd of senior boys gathered just inside the bathroom. All of this made Bede more self-conscious as he hurried through with taking his shower, while the senior boys all debated the pros and cons of what transpired the day before in the life of this fourteen-year-old school boy.

They began to disperse only as Bede got out of the shower, and he started to towel his body. "No signs," someone whispered.

"No wrinkles."

"No scars."

The prefect who caused this small gathering of senior boys spoke again. "All this should serve as a warning for everybody to be vigilant. We are being visited by spirits, it appears, that want to turn boys into old men."

"And to turn them back into boys again?" another senior boy asked.

"Yes. That is, if you're lucky enough to survive the first change. And there's no guaranteeing luck."

They looked at each other, and then chuckled to themselves.

In Sapele House, Bede Olo was dressing for the day. The sun was warming the campus fields. He would take a stroll into town and things would be fine. It would be a day to treasure.

And a day each of the other boys would remember for a very long time.

Review Requested:
If you loved this book, would you please provide a
review at Amazon.com?

CPSIA information can be obtained
at www.ICGtesting.com
Printed in the USA
BVHW031052170419
545784BV00001B/142/P